the vincent brothers

ALSO BY ABBI GLINES

The Vincent Boys

the vincent brothers

ABBI GLINES

Simon Pulse

New York   London   Toronto   Sydney   New Delhi

This book is a work of fiction. Any references to historical events, real people, or real places are used fictitiously. Other names, characters, places, and events are products of the author's imagination, and any resemblance to actual events or places or persons, living or dead, is entirely coincidental.

SIMON PULSE

An imprint of Simon & Schuster Children's Publishing Division
1230 Avenue of the Americas, New York, NY 10020
First Simon Pulse paperback edition December 2012
Copyright © 2011 by Abbi Glines

SIMON PULSE and colophon are registered trademarks of Simon & Schuster, Inc.
Also available in a Simon Pulse hardcover edition.
For information about special discounts for bulk purchases, please contact Simon & Schuster Special Sales at 1-866-506-1949 or business@simonandschuster.com.
The Simon & Schuster Speakers Bureau can bring authors to your live event. For more information or to book an event contact the Simon & Schuster Speakers Bureau at 1-866-248-3049 or visit our website at www.simonspeakers.com.
Designed by Mike Rosamilia
The text of this book was set in Adobe Caslon Pro.
Manufactured in the United States of America
2 4 6 8 10 9 7 5 3 1
This book is cataloged with the Library of Congress.
ISBN 978-1-4424-8529-7 (hc)
ISBN 978-1-4424-8528-0 (pbk)
ISBN 978-1-4424-8527-3 (eBook)

To Ava, my baby girl. Your smile makes everything better.
I'm so thankful that you're mine. Dream big, sweetheart,
and never settle for second best.

ACKNOWLEDGMENTS

I have to start by thanking Keith, my husband, who tolerated the dirty house, lack of clean clothes, and my mood swings, while I wrote this book (and all my other books).

My three precious kiddos, who ate a lot of corn dogs, pizza, and Frosted Flakes because I was locked away writing. I promise I cooked them many good hot meals once I finished.

I'd also like to thank my agent, Jane Dystel, who convinced me I needed an agent and taking a chance on me. She is brilliant, and I'm lucky to have her.

Jennifer Klonsky and the rest of the Simon Pulse staff have all been amazing through this process. As far as publishers go, it doesn't get any better.

Tammara Webber and Elizabeth Reyes, my critique

partners. Somehow, I convinced these ladies to become my critique partners. Now, I get to read their books before anyone else! I'd throw in an "I'm just kidding" but, well . . . I'm not. I love their work. It's a major perk. Both of them helped me so much with *The Vincent Brothers*. Their ideas, suggestions, and encouragement made the writing process so much easier. They're amazing, and I don't know how I ever finished a book without them.

My FP girls. I'm choosing not to share what FP stands for because my mother may read this and it will give her heart failure. Kidding . . . maybe. You girls make me laugh, listen to me vent, and always manage to give me some eye candy to make my day brighter. You are truly my posse.

Prologue

SAWYER

Ashton pulled herself up onto our branch and sat down. Once upon a time she'd needed me to give her a boost. Now she didn't need me for anything. I'd let her down in so many ways. I'd heard the term heartbreak before and never really understood it—until now. Sitting here, looking at her, my chest literally hurt. Taking a deep breath had become difficult since the day I'd walked outside the church and seen her with Beau. I'd known. I'd wanted her to tell me anything to prove me wrong. Still, deep down, I'd known. Ashton was no longer mine.

"Impressive. You made it look easy," I said loud enough so she could hear me. She'd texted me to tell me she was out here. I'd come down here to think hours ago. This was where it all started. It was fitting that it ended here too.

Ashton's expression was slightly confused. I loved that look. It was adorable. "I was here when you sent the text," I explained, and a small smile touched her lips.

"Oh," she replied.

"To what do I owe this visit?" I already had a good idea as to why she was here. I just wanted her to say it out loud. It was time we cleared the air for good. Standing up, I made my way over to where she sat on the limb, but not before I noticed the audience hidden in the darkness. It figured that Beau would come looking for me too. Or maybe he'd followed her.

"I wanted to check on you. Beau said you had a concussion."

I couldn't help but laugh. I had a concussion all right. I skipped a rock across the water. "He tell you how I got the concussion?"

"Yes." The guilt in her voice was thick. He must have admitted to bashing my head in. It wasn't her fault, though.

"I deserved it. I was shitty to you all week." My chest ached harder. Seeing everyone treat her so cruelly, while I sat back and did nothing, would haunt me for a long time.

"Um . . ." She seemed unsure of what to say next. I'd let her down. I'd let myself down. The guy I'd been, the way I'd reacted—that wasn't me.

"I shouldn't have let them do those things to you. Honestly, Beau beating the crap out of me was a relief. I'd been beating myself up. Having someone physically beat me was a nice release."

"What?"

She was surprised that I felt bad about what I'd let them do to her. *Damn,* if that didn't make this even harder. Breathing was becoming more difficult.

"Ash, you were my girl for years. Even before that, we were friends. The best of friends. I should've never let one bump in the road cause me to turn on you like I did. It was wrong. You took all the blame for something that wasn't entirely your fault. It was Beau's and it was mine."

"Yours? How—?"

"I knew Beau loved you. I'd seen the way he looked at you. I also knew you loved him, more than you did me. You two had a secret bond I didn't get to share. I was jealous. Beau was my cousin and you were the prettiest girl I'd ever seen. I wanted you for myself. So I asked you out. Without going to Beau first, never once asking him how he felt about it. You accepted and, just like magic, I broke up the bond you two had. Y'all never talked anymore. There were no more late-night roof talks and no more bailing y'all out of trouble. Beau was my family and you were my girlfriend. It was as if your friendship had never been. I was selfish and I ignored the guilt until it went away. Only, the times I saw him watching you, with that pained needy expression, did the guilt stir in my gut. It was mixed with fear. Fear you'd see what I'd done and go to him. Fear I'd lose you."

That was the first time I'd verbalized the truth. For years, I'd held it inside, even pushed it away when my conscience nagged at me. Watching Ashton transform her personality and never saying one word to stop her. All of it. This all was my fault.

Ashton's hand played lightly with my hair and I wanted to close my eyes and sigh from the small innocent touch. Would I always love her like this? Would I spend my life paying for my sin by living with the constant pain in my chest?

"I loved you, too. I wanted to be good enough for you. I wanted to be the good girl you deserved."

Hearing her say she'd wanted to be good enough for me reminded me once again why we hadn't worked out. She'd been perfect since the first day I'd met her, but I'd let her believe I expected more.

"Ash, you were perfect just the way you were. I was the one who let you change. I liked the change. It's one of the many reasons I feared I'd lose you. Deep down I knew one day that free spirit you'd quenched would fight for release. It happened. And the fact it happened with Beau doesn't surprise me in the least."

"I'm sorry, Sawyer. I never meant to hurt you. I made a mess of things. You aren't going to have to watch Beau and me together. I'm stepping out of both your lives. You can get back what was lost."

When Beau didn't come charging out of the woods cursing like a sailor, I knew he was too far back to hear us. I reached up and grabbed Ashton's hand. I was the only one who could convince her that she didn't need to do that. It was time I let her go.

"Don't do that, Ash. He needs you."

Shaking her head, she gave me a sad smile. "No, it's what he wants too. Today he hardly acknowledged me. He only spoke to me when he was making a point to everyone else; I was to be left alone."

She really didn't have a clue. "He won't last long. He's never been able to ignore you. Not even when he knew I was watching him. Right now he's dealing with a lot. And he's dealing with it alone. Don't push him away."

Jumping down from the limb, Ashton stood on her tiptoes and wrapped her arms around my neck for what I knew would be the last time. "Thank you. Your acceptance means the world to me. But right now he needs *you*. You're his brother. I'll just be a hindrance to you two dealing with everything."

The pain was almost unbearable now. Reaching out, I played with a lock of her hair. I'd been fascinated with its perfect golden color since we were five years old. She'd always reminded me of a fairy princess, even when she was baiting hooks with chicken livers. I'd lost my princess, but the memory of her was worth every sharp pain in my heart.

"Even if I was wrong to take you without a thought to Beau's feelings, I can't make myself regret it. I've had three amazing years with you, Ash."

That was my good-bye. Beau was out there waiting on me to walk away. It was his time now. I'd royally screwed up mine. Dropping her hair, I stepped back, turned, and walked into the woods toward my brother.

Chapter 1

Six months later . . .

SAWYER

I'd known better than to come here, but I couldn't keep avoiding the field parties. It was time I started acting as if Beau and Ash being together didn't bother me.

"Here, man." Ethan shoved a red plastic cup full of beer into my hand. Frowning, I started to hand it back to him. "Drink it. You need it. Hell, I need it just watching the three of you."

I was thankful he'd spoken low enough so that no one else could hear him. I could feel everyone sneaking glances at me. They were all waiting to see how I would react. It'd been six months since I'd lost Ash to my brother. It was easier to see them together now, but normally, I kept my distance. This was the first time I'd had to witness my horny ass brother kiss her neck, hand, head, and anything else he could get near his lips while he carried on a conversation with everyone else and Ashton snuggled up between his legs.

Ethan was right; I needed a drink. Touching the cup to my lips, I tilted my head back and took a very long gulp. Anything to distract me from the make-out session in front of me would be nice.

"I still can't believe you two aren't going to the same college. I always expected y'all to get signed on as a package deal." Toby Horn almost sounded letdown that I'd chosen to sign with the University of Florida instead of Alabama, like everyone expected me to. Beau and I had been planning to play for the Crimson Tide since we were five years old. But when Florida had offered me a full ride, I'd taken it. I needed the distance. Ashton was headed to Alabama with Beau, and I just couldn't do it too.

"Florida offered him a sweet deal. Can't blame him for taking it," Beau explained. He got it. He never mentioned it, but he knew why I'd gone with Florida. Beau had been careful for a long time not to shove his relationship with Ashton in my face, but since graduation he'd put that behind him. Every time I saw them lately, she was wrapped up in his arms and he was staring at her with that ridiculous worshipful expression he'd always reserved just for her.

"Alabama can't handle two Vincent boys. I needed to share the love," I replied, focusing my gaze on Toby before taking another swig of my beer.

"It's going to be weird not having you around, though," Ash said. *Damn.* Why'd she have to say anything? Couldn't she sit over there quietly and let Beau paw all over her? Hearing Ashton's voice made it impossible not to lift my eyes to meet her gaze.

The sad tilt of her full lips made that old familiar ache start up in my chest. Only Ashton could get to me this way. "You'll survive. Besides, you two hardly come up for air to notice much of anything else." I'd just sounded like an ass. Ashton's flinch from my snide comment was just another strike against me.

"Careful, Sawyer." The threat in Beau's voice was unmistakable. Silence fell over the group. Everyone's focus was on the two of us. The anger flashing in Beau's glare just pissed me off more. What did he have to be angry about? He had the girl.

"Why don't you calm down? I was responding to her comment. Am I not allowed to speak to her now?"

Beau gripped Ashton's waist and moved her away from him as he stood up. "You got a problem, Sawyer?"

Ashton scrambled to her feet, threw her arms around Beau's neck, and began begging him to ignore me, telling him I didn't mean anything by it, although we both knew I did. Beau's eyes never left mine as he reached behind his neck to unlatch Ashton's hold on him.

As I set my cup down on the bed of my truck, I took a step toward him. This was a fight I needed. Holding my aggression in was so damn hard at times. Ashton, however, wasn't having it. She grabbed Beau's shoulders and jumped up, wrapping her legs firmly around his waist. If seeing her wrapped around him didn't piss me off so bad, I'd laugh at her determination to keep us from fighting. She'd been dealing with us since we were kids, and she knew exactly how to keep us from coming to blows. Throwing herself in the line of fire was the only way.

Amusement lit Beau's eyes as his angry snarl turned into a pleased grin and his eyes shifted from me to Ashton. "What ya doin', baby?" he asked in that slow drawl I hated. He'd been using it on girls since we hit puberty.

"That's the way to distract him, Ash," hooted Kayla Jenkins from Toby's lap.

More catcalls and whistles started. Beau was smiling at her now like she was the most fascinating person in the world. That was it for me. I had to get out of there.

"Let's go get something to eat—I'm starved," Ethan suggested, and Jake North agreed.

"You drive," Ethan called out, and climbed into the passenger seat of my truck. Without looking back at Ash and Beau, I walked around my truck and hopped in. If he hauled her off to his truck, I'd lose it. Leaving was the best idea.

LANA

Jewel flirted outrageously with the bartender. I knew her game and was willing to bet he did too. The brilliant scheme to flash cleavage and bat eyelashes while giggling wasn't the most original idea ever concocted. Why she couldn't just be happy with her soda while we waited for a table was beyond me. The ten-hour road trip I'd been on with her from Alpharetta, Georgia, to southern Alabama fulfilled my quota on quality time spent with my childhood friend and next-door neighbor. Jewel and I had grown up and become two completely different people, but that bond from our childhood had somehow kept us from drifting apart. Still, Jewel could only be endured in small doses.

"Come on, Lana, flash him a view of those fabulous boobs you've finally decided to share with the world," Jewel whispered as her gaze stayed on the young guy fixing drinks for another customer. Shaking my head at her ridiculous request, I picked up my soda and took a sip. I was happy with my soda. If she wanted to make a fool out of herself in hopes of getting a mixed drink, then fine, but I wasn't about to join in. The last thing I needed was to get caught with an alcoholic drink only thirty minutes away from my aunt and uncle's house. My uncle was a Baptist preacher, and if he found out I'd been drinking alcohol, there was no way he'd let me stay with him and his family for the summer.

"You're such a party pooper, Lana," Jewel whined, and glared at my drink like it was offensive.

I didn't really care if she was upset at this point. I just wanted to get some dinner and then get to my aunt and uncle's. The sight of Jewel's taillights driving away was going to be a welcome event.

"I don't get you, Lana. You go and get all gorgeous and finally decide to flaunt what your momma—okay, maybe not your momma because God knows she ain't real attractive; how about flaunt what luck must have given you?—and for what? Nothing! That's what! You buy yourself a new, sexy, cute wardrobe and get a hairstyle to show off that head of hair of yours, but you *never* flirt. It's as if you did this for yourself, and that's just dumb. Guys notice you now, Lana. They turn their heads, but you just ignore them."

This was a familiar tirade of hers. It drove her nuts that I didn't throw myself at any boy who looked my way. I wasn't about to tell her the reason why. That kind of information would make Jewel dangerous. She'd find a way to ruin everything. She wouldn't mean to, of course, but she would. Her loud mouth always seemed to bring a world of trouble with it.

"I've told you that I'm just not interested in dating right now. We just graduated. I want a summer to prepare for college in the fall, enjoy being away from my insane mother, and just—relax."

Jewel sighed and bent her head down to nibble on her straw while her eyes zeroed in on the poor bartender who must have been about ready for us to be seated at a table.

"You can still come with me, you know. Skip this living-with-the-preacher stuff and come party all summer at the beach. Corey would love you to join us. Her stepfather's condo has three bedrooms and a killer view of the ocean."

A summer hanging out with a drunken Jewel and friends was not appealing at all. I had my plans, and so far everything I'd put into motion was running smoothly. But I couldn't help but be nervous about the next step. It was the most crucial.

Having my naturally red hair darkened to a deep copper and styled attractively instead of pulled back in a braid or ponytail had been step one. The darker red color had made my pale skin seem almost delicate. Then the cleaning out of my closet had been the next move. I'd bagged up every single piece of clothing I owned and dropped it off at the local Goodwill. My mother had been horrified, but after she'd seen the clothing style I intended to replace it with, she'd been very supportive. Unlike most mothers, my mother wanted to see me in shorts that showed off almost all my legs and tight tops that emphasized my c-cup boobs.

Jewel had wanted to teach me how to apply makeup, but I'd kindly refused and went to the Clinique counter at Macy's and had them teach me. Then I'd bought everything they'd used. Although I'd never been one for makeup, I had to agree that it did startling things to my eyes. I'd closed my bedroom door and stared at myself in fascination for hours after they'd put makeup on me.

Convincing my mother to let me stay the summer with my aunt and uncle had been a little more difficult. My cousin Ashton had helped tremendously with this part. She'd talked to her mother who in return talked to mine. Our mothers are sisters, and once my aunt convinced my mother that Ashton truly wanted me to come spend our last summer before college together, I'd been so excited I'd momentarily forgotten about the last step in the plan, the reason why I'd made myself moderately attractive and begged to come stay the summer with my cousin. The goal sounded so simple, but when I allowed myself to dwell on it then, it became so incredibly complicated. Getting a boy to fall head-over-heels in love with you wasn't easy—especially when he'd been in love with your cousin for as long as you could remember.

Chapter 2

SAWYER

"You've got to curb the temper, man. If anyone could take on Beau, it would be you, but you'd still walk away beat-up," Ethan announced as I pulled out onto the country road from the dirt one that led back to the field party.

"It's been six months, bro. How long you gonna be pissed over this?" Jake asked from the backseat.

Why was this any of their business? Neither one of them knew what a committed relationship was like. They'd both been through so many girls during our four years of high school that I couldn't even name them all. Explaining to them that from the time I was twelve years old, I'd planned my life with Ashton at the center wasn't exactly easy. So instead I leaned forward and turned on the radio to drown out any more of their interrogations.

"You can turn on music all you want, but the fact is you got to let this go," Ethan said. "He's your cousin and your best friend. A chick can't come between that. Not for long." Ethan was watching me from the passenger seat. I knew he was waiting for a response from me, but I didn't give him one. His comment about Beau being my cousin was reminder enough that no one really knew me—except Beau and Ash. Beau wasn't my cousin; he was my brother. But once he found out the truth from his mother, he'd decided to keep that information locked away where it'd been his whole life. He didn't want to claim my dad as his own, and I couldn't really blame him. It wasn't like my dad had ever done anything to help Beau's home situation growing up. Beau held nothing but disdain for my father—*our* father. He chose to remember our father's brother as his dad. He'd been the only dad Beau had ever known. Even though he'd died when Beau was in first grade, he'd been a fond memory for Beau—unlike his real father.

"Hey! You passed Hank's," Ethan announced, pointing his finger toward the burger place where we normally went to eat.

"Not going to Hank's" was my only response. *They* were the ones who jumped in my truck. If they didn't like my need to get out of Grove, then they could walk back to town when we got to where I was headed.

"You leaving Grove?" Jake asked.

"Yep."

Ethan sighed and leaned back in his seat. "We may end up in Florida before he stops this damn truck."

"Florida? I'm starving, and a cheeseburger from Hank's would've fixed that," Jake grumbled.

Slowing down the truck, I pulled over and glanced back at Jake. "You're welcome to get out and walk back."

His eyes widened and he slowly shook his head. "No, man, that's okay. I'm good."

I pulled back onto the road and ignored the exchange between the guys. They both thought I was nursing a broken heart. Well, they were right.

No one said another word until I pulled the truck into the parking lot of Wings. I'd driven about twenty miles south to the next town big enough for decent restaurants.

"You should've told me you were headed to Wings. I'd have shut up." Jake made an excited whoop as he jerked open the back door of the truck and jumped out.

This was somewhere I'd never eaten with Ash. There weren't many places where I didn't have a memory of her, so my choices were limited. Tonight I needed to get my mind off her and focus on my future—or at least my summer.

"I'm gonna eat my weight in some wings," Ethan said in reply to Jake's excitement over my choice of restaurant. At least I'd made them happy. Not that it mattered.

Opening the door, I went inside and stopped at the hostess stand. A tall girl with long, blond hair pulled back in a ponytail smiled up at me with an appreciative gleam in her eye that I was used to. It had been habit for me to ignore that look in other girls' eyes for so long that I automatically brushed it off. Tonight I wasn't going to do that. It was time I started flirting back.

I flashed a grin that I knew was pretty damn impressive because it was the one Ashton always commented on. "Three please," I told her, and watched as her brown eyes got bigger and she blinked several times. She wasn't exceptionally pretty, but seeing her get all flustered was a nice boost to my ego.

"Oh . . . um . . . okay . . . y-yes . . . uh," she stammered, reaching for the menus and instead knocking them to the floor.

I bent down beside her to help pick them up.

"I'm sorry. I'm not normally so clumsy," she explained, two bright red splotches of color staining her cheeks.

"So it's just me then?" I teased.

A nervous giggle erupted from her, and I realized she'd never do. I didn't like giggles. Ash wasn't a giggler.

Handing her the menus, I stood back up and pointedly shifted my attention elsewhere. I didn't need to flirt with her anymore. She'd get the wrong idea.

"Okay, um, this way," I heard her say. Both Ethan and Jake quickly fell in behind her. I started to follow when my gaze stopped its uninterested appraisal of the bar to focus in on a female I would happily let giggle all she wanted.

Auburn hair hung down her back and curled on the ends. Two very long, bare legs were crossed as she sat on the barstool and a silver, backless, high-heeled sandal dangled off the toe of a very dainty foot. I hadn't seen the face of this one yet but from the back, she was a head-turner. She had major potential.

"You coming or what?" Jake yelled, but I didn't turn my head to see how far they'd gone or where they were being seated. Instead I stood, frozen, watching her. Jake's loud voice caught her attention, and she turned in her seat and glanced over her shoulder toward him. Her creamy, smooth complexion was dotted with freckles. Normally, I wasn't a fan of a lot of freckles, but the bedroom look to her green eyes and the full, almost unreal-looking lips made it all work. She started to turn back around after seeing what the yelling had been about when she stopped and her eyes locked with mine.

Surprise, pleasure, and anxiety all flittered across her face as she studied me. I was fascinated. The bartender came up behind her and said something. She glanced back at him.

"Sawyer, man, come on," Ethan called out this time. Tearing my gaze from the redhead, I made my way to the table where the hostess was standing with our menus.

"Sawyer, wait." A familiar voice stopped me in my tracks. Disbelief settled over me as I turned back around to see the pretty redhead making her way toward me. As I made my way up her body, appreciating the view, I noticed a short, denim skirt that stopped several inches above her knees. The white top she was wearing tied at her waist in some sort of loose knot and small glimpses of a flat, smooth stomach peeked out as she moved. Finally I managed to get my focus off the impressive cleavage the shirt displayed in order to see her face. A small smile tugged on those ridiculously plump lips and recognition dawned on me.

No fucking way.

"Lana?" The incredulity in my voice was unmistakable. The last person I'd expected to see was Ashton's cousin. The fact she was the girl I'd been checking out was even more shocking.

"Sawyer," she replied, a full grin on her face.

"What're you doing here?" I asked, thinking more along the lines of *What the hell happened to you?* She looked nothing like the girl I'd seen about seven or so months ago. That girl had been sweet, prim, and proper. This one in front of me was a walking sexual fantasy.

"Eating," she quipped, and I realized I was smiling. A real smile, not a forced one, for the first time in months.

"Well, yeah, I kind of gathered that. I meant, what are you doing here, in southern Alabama?" She pressed her lips together, and then her tongue peeked out and nervously licked them. *Hmmm. . . I wouldn't mind tasting those lips either.*

"I'm staying with Ashton this summer. My friend is headed to the beach, so she's dropping me off at Ash's after we eat."

Ash. Damn. Did she have to bring up Ashton? My good mood evaporated, and once again I was forcing a smile. She glanced over my shoulder at my friends' table and frowned.

"You guys are already seated at a table?" She shot her frustrated gaze over toward the hostess stand. "Figures," she muttered. I followed her gaze and saw the blond hostess watching us with an irritated frown on her face.

"What's wrong?" I asked, turning my attention back to Lana.

She sighed and looked back at me. "We've been waiting on a table for at least fifteen minutes."

Ah. The waitress had given us their table. I could fix this problem.

"Go get your friend, and y'all come sit with us."

Lana flashed a bright smile. "Okay, thanks. I'll be right back."

I watched as she spun around and walked back to the bar. Her backside was impossible not to watch as her hips swayed gently from side to side. *Damn.* Lana looked good.

LANA

"Oh my god, did you just *flirt* with that hottie? Dang, girl, when you decide to flaunt it, you shoot high." The awe in Jewel's voice made me want to laugh. But the fact I felt like I was about to throw up kept the humor at bay. Sawyer had checked me out. His eyes had slowly scanned my body. He'd paused at my boobs. I felt the need to fan myself with the stupid coaster under my drink.

"I know him. And we're sitting with him and his friends," I announced, reaching for my purse and soda.

"Really?" Jewel squealed happily, snatching her purse from the seat beside her and standing up. The scarf thing she called a shirt showed off all of her flat, tanned stomach. The bar in her belly button flashed two small rhinestones on each end, causing eyes to immediately focus on her exposed skin. Then the Daisy Duke's she was wearing made my miniskirt look classy. The girl turned heads when she walked, if for no other reason than because most of her body was on display.

"Come on," I snapped, and headed toward Sawyer, who was standing right where I'd left him, waiting on us. His eyes drifted over to Jewel, and I watched him appraise her the same way he had appraised me. A sick knot formed in my stomach, and I fought the urge to push her behind me. I didn't want him doing that slow, sexy trek up her body with his eyes.

"He's so freaking hot," Jewel hissed beside me. She'd stuck out her chest farther, and the flip thing she did over her shoulders with her long, blond hair had just happened. She was getting ready to unleash her skills on Sawyer.

"Not him, Jewel. Pick one of the others. Just not him." I

tried not to sound like I was begging, but there was no masking the desperation in my voice.

I heard a small gasp beside me.

"He's the reason you . . ." She trailed off as her mind wrapped around what she was just now figuring out. "Oh, wow. I get it. I won't poach," she replied.

No, but she was still tanned, freckle-free, blond, and well practiced in the world of men. Those were all things Sawyer liked.

When we reached him, as much as I hated it, I knew I had to make introductions. *Why hadn't I just left her at the bar to flirt with the bartender and pretended like she didn't exist?* Sawyer's appreciative gaze was locked on Jewel, and although she'd promised me she wouldn't flirt, it was ingrained in her. The girl couldn't help it.

"Hi, I'm Jewel," she drawled out in a sexy voice that had me wanting to slap her stupid.

"It's nice to meet you, Jewel," he replied, taking her hand in his large one and . . . *Did he just squeeze it?* "I'm Sawyer. An old friend of Lana's."

The fact that I was leaving them to make their own introductions wasn't lost on me. I just couldn't open my mouth; I was afraid I'd let out the angry snarl vibrating in my throat. At the moment, I really hated Jewel. She was going to spend her summer with a guy that was supposed to be her boyfriend, but she was unleashing all her charms to get what out of Sawyer? A one-nighter? I shivered at the thought. I just might have killed her if she'd dared.

"Lana?" Sawyer's voice startled me from my vicious thoughts, and I blinked several times to clear my head.

"Um, yes, I'm sorry," I replied.

"She's exhausted from the trip," Jewel explained, covering for me. No doubt she knew what was wrong.

"I asked if you wanted me to drive you back to Ashton's after we eat so that Jewel doesn't have to."

Oh, he is offering me a ride. Jewel would be gone. *Yes, please.*

"That would be great. Thanks." I managed to keep the excitement out of my voice.

A pleased smile touched his lips, and I wanted to reach over and feel them, see if they were as smooth as they looked. How weird was that?

Sawyer led the way over to the booth where two other guys were smiling up at us. You could see the surprised curiosity in their eyes.

"Guys, this is Lana, Ash's cousin, and her friend Jewel. They were waiting on a table and I offered to share ours." Sawyer turned back to us. "The guy to the left is Ethan, and the guy to the right is Jake."

Ethan had a nice smile and short, dark hair. It was just barely long enough to flip up some in the front. His dark brown eyes appeared warm and amused. I liked him instantly. I needed to pick a side of the half-circle booth to slide into, and he seemed to be the less threatening of the two. Taking a quick peek at Jake, I saw he was drinking in Jewel's bare stomach with his gaze. The blond curls peeking out of his baseball cap were cute, but the sexual gleam in his gray eyes was a little unnerving.

"Jewel," Sawyer said, motioning for her to slide in on Jake's side. I moved to slide in on Ethan's side. I felt extremely grateful; I wouldn't have to sit beside Jake.

Then I watched as Sawyer slid in behind Jewel. My stomach dropped. He'd had to pick a side, and without a second thought he'd chosen Jewel's. His offer to drive me to Ashton's now seemed unimportant. He'd done it to be considerate because that's what he was. Not because he had been attracted to me or even remotely interested. I was an idiot.

"I didn't know Ash had a cousin," Ethan said. I tore my eyes off Sawyer as he sidled up to Jewel and focused on the guy beside me. At least he didn't look upset about getting stuck with me instead of Jewel.

"Um, yes, I'm the only one. I live in Georgia and get down to visit her about once a year, at the most."

Ethan's easy smile showcased straight white teeth. I liked good teeth on a guy. And Ethan wasn't bad to look at either. His dark eyes were outlined with really long lashes.

"So, you staying long?"

"All summer," I replied. Ethan's smile looked approving and he nodded his head.

"Nice," he said, then lifted his gaze to the waitress who'd just walked up.

"What can I get y'all to drink?" she asked, tucking a strand of brown hair behind her ear and forcing a smile that didn't match her eyes.

"Coke," Ethan announced, then glanced down at my almost-empty one. "Make that two Cokes."

He'd ordered for me. I liked that. No guy had ever ordered for me. It made me feel oddly special.

"A screwdriver for me," Jewel said, as if she was going to get away with this. I glared at her and she gave me a small smirk.

"ID," the waitress replied, and this time *I* smirked as Jewel immediately went from looking cocky to looking irritated.

"Don't have it with me," she replied in an annoyed tone.

"I bet you don't," the waitress muttered.

"Are you saying I don't look twenty-one?" Jewel asked, as if she was shocked someone would even question it. Because, of course, an eighteen-year-old girl could pass for twenty-one easily. Whatever.

"Yes, that's what I'm saying," the waitress deadpanned.

Jewel opened her mouth to argue, no doubt, and I knew I needed to step in and stop her before we all got thrown out.

"Just bring her a Diet Coke, please," I told the waitress with an apologetic smile. Then I sent a warning glare over toward Jewel.

She harrumphed and crossed her arms over her chest in a pout. Luckily, she didn't have much in the way of cleavage, so Sawyer wasn't leering down her shirt as she pushed her small boobs up with her ridiculous posture.

Everyone else ordered their drinks. Sawyer leaned down to whisper something to Jewel that made her giggle, and I decided I needed to focus on the menu and just get through this. I don't know why I'd hoped for anything different.

"You handled that well," Ethan whispered, opening his menu beside me. I peeked over at him and smiled. "Thanks. It happens a lot."

He grinned and studied his menu. I did the same.

Chapter 3

SAWYER

If that girl giggled one more time, I was going to rip off pieces of my napkin and shove them in my ears. *Damn*, she was annoying. When I'd first seen her, I'd thought she could potentially distract me from Ashton tonight, but I'd been so very wrong. All she was managing to do was get on my nerves. If her hand slid up my thigh one more time, I was going to end up pushing her toward Jake.

Soft laughter caught my attention, and I turned to Lana. She was smiling brightly at whatever Ethan was saying to her. He'd been talking to her in whispered tones throughout the entire meal. That was grating on my nerves as well. Ever since she sat down beside him, he'd taken up all her attention. It was as if the rest of us weren't even at the damn table.

"Looks like she's interested in your friend," Jewel said, obviously noting where my attention was focused.

"Hmmm" was my only response.

"How long have you known Lana?" she asked. I thought back to the days of her bright orange ponytails and skinny legs with knobby knees and realized she'd come a very long way. Those freckles that had once made her unattractive now somehow enhanced her looks.

"Since we were kids. I always used to have to take up for her with Ash and Beau. They tormented her."

"Beau?" Jewel asked. Apparently, Lana didn't talk much about Ashton to her friend. If she did, she'd know exactly who Beau was.

"My br—uh, cousin," I replied.

Lana threw her head back and let out a real laugh this time. Not one she was trying to silence, but one that meant she was thoroughly delighted about something and didn't care who heard her. Her long, silky, auburn locks brushed the edge of the table, and I wondered how she'd react if I wrapped one of those locks around my finger.

"You think that's funny, huh?" Ethan replied, grinning like an idiot because he'd made her laugh so hard.

Lana nodded her head, reached out, and squeezed his arm. "Yes, I do. I'm sorry," she replied, trying to keep the huge grin off her face.

Ethan's body language said he didn't mind at all as he leaned into her touch and began that damn whispering again. Those two were lost in their own little world.

"She isn't normally good with guys. They make her nervous," Jewel pointed out.

She didn't look nervous to me, although I had to agree that the Lana I remembered was quiet and reserved. What had changed other than the fact that she had gone from forgettable to gorgeous in a few short months?

Jake said something to Jewel, and she turned her attention to him. Finally I had some relief. Maybe she would grope his thigh now and leave mine alone.

Lana reached for her drink and her eyes met mine. She paused briefly, then smiled at me. She really had a nice smile. And those freckles . . . *Damn*, they were cute.

"Enjoying your dinner?" I asked.

She snuck a peek over at Ethan, who was still staring at her like a lovesick puppy. She'd managed to wrap him around her little finger rather quickly. "Yes, thank you," she replied, then took a sip of her drink. Those lush lips wrapped around the straw, and I had to swallow hard to keep from groaning. How had little Lana McDaniel become so skilled in the ways of seducing a man?

"Lana mentioned we were giving her a ride to Ashton's," Ethan said, and I tore my gaze off Lana and her straw to glare at him. Why I was glaring, I wasn't sure. He'd done nothing wrong. He'd entertained Lana and made sure she felt comfortable at the table. Forcing my face to relax, I nodded. "Yeah, I figured since we were going that way, I could take her and Jewel could continue on toward the beach."

Ethan appeared a little too pleased. "Good idea," he replied with a smile, and leaned over to say something to Lana that caused her to grin.

Paying for the meal and getting out of there had been my number one priority. I was ready to send Jewel on her way. Girls who didn't take a hint annoyed me. I signed the receipt and stuck my debit card back in my wallet.

"Here," Jewel said in an unhappy tone as she handed the waitress her receipt and a twenty-dollar bill.

"Ethan, *no*." Lana's voice broke into my thoughts, and I watched as she frowned up at Ethan, who in return was grinning.

"I need out. I've got to go to the restroom before I hit the road again," Jewel said. I stood up and let her by but didn't take my eyes off Lana and Ethan, who appeared to be arguing—or at least Lana looked like she was arguing and Ethan was enjoying himself.

"Those two are about to make me gag," Jake muttered, getting out of the booth. "Besides, why the hell would he go and pay for the chick's meal if he just met her? It ain't like this is a date."

He'd paid for her meal? *Why hadn't I thought of that?* It was the polite thing to do. She was Ash's cousin. I should have paid for it. Except, I'd been so focused on getting away from Jewel that I hadn't thought of anything else.

"Come on, E., let's roll." Jake didn't try to mask his annoyance. He must have struck out with Jewel.

Lana quickly scooted out of the booth and stood up. Ethan was right behind her with her small red purse in his hand.

"You forgot this," he said as he stepped behind her.

Lana flashed him a grateful smile and thanked him.

Stalking toward the door, I didn't glance back to see if anyone was following me. I needed to get outside and get some fresh air before I went off on someone for absolutely no reason.

LANA

Sawyer was quiet. I tried not to stare at him as he and Ethan took my things from Jewel's car and loaded them in the back of Sawyer's truck. He seemed in a hurry to leave. Maybe Jewel had laid it on a little too thick and he was ready to get away from her. The thought made me smile.

Peeking over at him through the veil of my hair, I could see he'd relaxed since we'd gotten in the truck. Ethan had offered Jake the front seat and said he'd sit with me in the extended cab, but Sawyer had said he wasn't making me crawl into the back of the truck. I didn't really consider sitting in the roomy cab with the comfortable seat "crawling" into anything, but I hadn't argued. His angry scowl had made me scramble into the front. Thankfully, he'd seemed to calm down once the other two got into the back.

"You can change the station if you want," Sawyer said, glancing in my direction.

I hadn't been paying any attention to what was on the radio. I'd been more worried about figuring out why he was being so surly all of a sudden. This wasn't the Sawyer I remembered. Normally, he was all smiles and politeness. This must be Sawyer after Ashton. The thought made me sad.

"Ah, man, don't let her choose. She's a chick. She'll pick some awful boy band shit," Jake complained from the backseat. "Umph, ow, what the hell?" he snapped. I turned to see Ethan glaring at him.

If only Sawyer liked me as much as Ethan obviously did. Then again, Ethan was more in my league.

"I've a good mind to let her crawl back there and slap you," Sawyer said with an amused tone to his voice.

"S'okay. I think E. bruised my ribs. I'll shut up."

The rest of the trip was pretty uneventful. There wasn't much talking, except for Sawyer asking me if I was comfortable.

He'd turned the air vent toward me and told me to close it if I got cold. He'd changed the channels several times and always asked if I liked that song. This was the Sawyer I was used to: the attentive, polite one. Not the moody guy I'd witnessed all night.

When Sawyer pulled onto the dirt road that I knew led to the field parties, I searched the parking lot for Ashton's car or Beau's truck. I wasn't sure I was ready to witness Ashton with both of the Vincent boys just yet. If Sawyer was still hung up on her, it would almost kill me.

"I'll see y'all later. I'm going to go ahead and take Lana to Ash's."

Ethan cleared his throat, drawing my attention from the parked vehicles to him.

"Uh, I can take her," he said in a cautious tone as he stared at Sawyer. Sawyer, on the other hand, hadn't even turned around to look at him.

"I got this, Ethan," he replied in a cool, hard voice.

Ethan shifted his gaze from me to Sawyer, then let out a defeated sigh and opened the door and got out.

Once he'd closed the door, Sawyer backed up and turned around. I was silently thrilled he'd wanted to take me to Ashton's, but then the nagging reminder that he was probably doing it in hopes of seeing Ashton squelched my joy.

Instead of torturing myself with different scenarios in my

head, I decided to ask him about Ashton.

"So how are things with the three of you?" I didn't have to elaborate. I knew he would know exactly who I was talking about.

He tensed up, then let out a breath and cocked his head to the side and cut his eyes toward me. "Would you believe me if I said we were doing great?" The sad smile on his face broke my heart.

"No," I replied.

He let out a small chuckle and ran his hand through his dark hair. "You knew about them last time you were here, didn't you? I remember that time at the field party. Something had been off about that whole scenario. For starters, you aren't Beau's type, and Ash wouldn't have gotten all worked up if he had flirted with you, because they'd mended their fences." He shook his head. "Guess you were the only reason I believed that story. I didn't figure you for a liar."

I always knew that lie was going to come back to haunt me. When Sawyer had found Ashton and Beau having a lover's spat, I couldn't stand the thought of Sawyer finding out the truth that way. So I'd lied and told Sawyer that Beau had hit on me and Aston didn't think he was good enough for me. I'd told Ashton later that she had to choose one Vincent boy or let them both go because what she was doing to Sawyer was wrong.

"I'm sorry," I replied—because I was.

Sawyer nodded. "Yeah, me too."

The rest of the drive over to Ashton's was fairly quiet. He didn't ask me if I was comfortable, and he didn't turn on the radio. *Why had I opened my big mouth?* Reminding him about my part in his cousin and girlfriend's deception had been stupid.

"Ash's car is here, but I doubt she's home. She was with Beau at the field earlier."

I nodded and reached for the door handle. I'd said enough tonight. I needed to get out of his truck before I said anything else stupid.

"Wait, Lana." Sawyer's hand reached out, and his fingers wrapped around my upper arm. Goose bumps popped out all over my skin from the touch of his rough warm skin.

"Uh, yeah," I managed to choke out.

"Look, I was a jerk. I'm sorry. It isn't your fault. That crap with Ash and Beau, none of it was your fault. I just needed an outlet to vent, and you were the only person around. I was wrong. . . ." He paused, and I glanced back at him. "Forgive me?"

The sincere look in his eyes made me melt. He was like a sweet wounded puppy. Ashton had been crazy to hurt him. *I mean, who does that?* He was so perfect. *How can you hurt someone so incredibly perfect?*

"Yes, of course."

A smile lit up his face. He squeezed my arm then let go. "Phew, thank you."

We both got out of the truck, and I met him on the other side. I reached for the luggage he was lifting out of the back and setting on the driveway.

"I'll help you. Don't get the heavy stuff," Sawyer said as he grabbed the last bag. I didn't normally pack so much, but now that I wore makeup and styled my hair and had an actual wardrobe, I had quite a few pieces of luggage.

"Thanks."

"I didn't peg you as a girl who packs a lot," he observed.

I shrugged. "Things change." I reached down to pick up my cosmetic and toiletry bags. They were two of the smaller ones.

"Yeah, they do, don't they?" His gaze shifted back to the house, and I knew he was staring up at Ashton's window. He was so not over her.

"She's an idiot . . . for what it's worth." I would have slapped my hand over my mouth if both of my hands weren't already full. I couldn't believe I'd just said that.

Sawyer swung his attention back to me. His dark eyebrows arched in surprise at my statement, and I was sure my cheeks were bright red.

"You think so?"

Well, I can't exactly deny it now. So I nodded.

Sawyer took a step closer to me, and my heart was beating so hard against my chest I felt the need to gasp for air. His green eyes studied me carefully. It was as if he were looking at me for the first time. His eyes dropped to my mouth, and I fought the urge to lick my lips nervously.

"You think I'm a better choice than Beau? He's the bad one, you know. The dangerous one. Girls like bad boys." His voice had dropped to a low rumble. I shivered as he took another step closer, his eyes never leaving their study of my lips. It had been a while since I'd reapplied lip gloss. I wondered if my lips were dry.

Forcing myself to remain calm, I responded, "Not all girls."

"Hmmm ..."

He raised his hand and gently ran the pad of his thumb over my bottom lip. I mentally imagined biting his thumb and pulling it into my mouth to suck it, but I didn't. Instead I just stopped breathing.

"They are as soft as they look . . . maybe softer," he whispered, then he lowered his head and before I could take a calming breath, his mouth was on mine.

Forcing oxygen into my lungs via my nose, I dropped both the bags in my hands and grabbed on to his arms to keep from passing out due to the overwhelming fact I was actually being kissed by Sawyer Vincent.

His hands settled on my waist and gently squeezed the bare skin they touched. I think I may have moaned when he pulled my bottom lip into his mouth to suck on it. Before I could completely throw myself at him, he was gone. Dizzy and completely shaken, I lost my balance and reached out to grab the side of the truck.

"Whoa." Sawyer's hand shot out to steady me.

Now that was embarrassing. I took a steadying breath and lifted my eyes—once I was able to focus them again—to look at Sawyer. Instead of having an awestruck expression like I was sure I had plastered on my face, he was frowning. No—make that scowling.

"I shouldn't have done that, Lana. I'm sorry. I was upset and I just didn't think." He reached down and grabbed my two heavy suitcases and headed for the front door without waiting for me to respond.

That hadn't been the way I'd pictured our first kiss ending. And trust me, I'd been fantasizing about that kiss for years. Most of my life. Although the kiss itself was spot-on perfect, the ending was way off course.

Anger suddenly took the place of disappointment, and I snatched up the remaining bags and followed him. *How dare he kiss me like that, then apologize and walk off?*

"That's—"

The front door swung open, ending my sentence, which was probably a good thing since I was about to let him have it.

"Lana, sweetheart, you're here." Aunt Sarah beamed at me as she pushed the screen door open.

Shooting Sawyer an angry glare, I rushed past him and into the house.

Chapter 4

SAWYER

That couldn't be good. I mentally cursed myself for making such a jackass move. Jerking my truck door open, I started to climb inside when Beau's truck pulled in behind me. Perfect. Not what I needed right then. I needed to wrap my head around that stupid kiss with Lana—not face Beau and Ash.

Beau's truck door swung open, and he got out with an angry snarl on his face. What was his deal?

"Better be a damn good reason you're parked in Ash's drive."

Adjusting to Beau being a caveman over a girl had been almost as hard as seeing him with Ash. Beau hadn't done jealous until Ashton had become his. Then he became a freaking lunatic.

"I just dropped Lana off," I replied, meeting his angry glare.

I wasn't scared of his stupid tough-guy shit. I'd been in more fights with him than I could count.

My answer obviously confused him because he raised one eyebrow and turned to look at Ash as she scooted out behind him on the driver's side.

"She's here?" Ash squealed, jumping down before Beau could catch her. "Remember I told you Lana was coming tonight?" She beamed up at Beau, then frowned and looked over at me. "Why . . . How did *you* get her?"

Ash was adorable when she was confused. "She was eating dinner at Wings when we stopped in to eat," I said. "I offered to give her a ride to save her friend the trip."

Ashton's frown turned up into a smile again. I liked making her smile—I always had. "Thank you! I'm so glad you met up with her." Ash turned and wrapped her arms around Beau and laid a loud, quick kiss on his lips before releasing him and stepping back. "I gotta go see her. I haven't seen her in months. Call me later."

Beau grabbed her hand and turned it palm up before kissing it and then licking it. *Gross, I do not want to see this,* I thought. "Yeah, I'll call you when I crawl into bed." His had voice dropped until it was much deeper than normal and I swore I heard Ashton sigh. I'd seen more than I had wanted. I started to climb up into my truck.

"Sawyer, wait." Beau's command stopped me. I really just wanted to leave, but he was blocking me in so I couldn't exactly escape.

Ashton ran inside, and once she closed the door, Beau turned his gaze toward me.

"About tonight. Don't do that again. It's been six months, and Ashton goes out of her way to be kind to you. You talk to her that way again, and I'm gonna kick your ass."

Figures it wasn't an apology but a threat. But he was right; I had been a jerk to Ashton. I didn't want to push either of them away. They both knew me better than anyone did; they'd been my best friends all my life. We shared a secret, and we shared memories. Both formed a bond so important that I'd given up Ash without much of a fight in order to preserve them.

"You're right. I was a jackass. I'll apologize to her next time I see her."

Beau seemed appeased. His eyes shifted back to her now-lit bedroom window. She and Lana would be inside talking, and I wondered if I'd have something else to apologize for the next time I saw her. Because if Lana told her about that kiss, Ash would be pissed. Not because I had kissed Lana, but because I'd been a complete dick afterward.

"Good." Beau started to get into his truck, but stopped. "Hey, you wanna go play some pool?"

"Aunt Honey working?"

"Yep."

That meant free beer. I nodded. "Lead the way."

* * *

LANA

I'd barely made it inside the door when Ashton came racing inside, squealing. She'd made quick work of getting us past her parents and their questions concerning my parents, and up to her room. She closed the door and spun around, smiling brightly at me.

"I am so glad you're here."

Her long, blond hair was hanging loose down her back, and her golden tan was already perfect. How did she do that? It had been summer for what now? A week? We shared the same green eyes. That was it. When I was younger, I'd hated her. Not because she was mean, but because she looked like a Barbie doll. To retaliate, I'd been the one who was mean.

"Me too," I replied as she plunked down on the bed beside me. Getting away from my mother and her endless griping about my dad was a major relief. They'd been officially divorced now for three months, but she still ranted about him daily.

"We're going to have so much fun. Kayla Jenkins's birthday is tomorrow night, and she's having a huge party at her house. She throws one every year. You'll love it, and you'll get to meet everyone. Then Beau and I have been talking about a camping trip. Maybe for a week up at Cheaha State Park. We're going to invite Sawyer, since hiking is his thing, plus some other people. You, of course, are coming too. And Leann is at the beach all summer at her grandmother's beach house. So I told her we'd come visit her one week."

Forcing a smile was hard, but I somehow managed. And pushing Sawyer's reaction to our kiss as far away from my mind as I could, I put all my focus into talking to Ashton.

"That all sounds like fun. I'm game for whatever," I assured her.

Leaning forward she touched my hair and studied my face. Then her face broke into a huge grin. "You're wearing makeup and your hair is darker and"—she studied my skirt and top—"you have stylish clothes."

"I decided it was time for a change," I replied, unable to suppress my smile.

"Well, you look *hot*."

Ashton stood up and started pulling off the cowboy boots she'd been wearing. She'd pair them with a black sundress that barely made it halfway to her knees. It was like God had decided to try his hand at making someone perfect and chose Ashton as his experiment.

"Sawyer said he brought you home. How was he? I mean, was he in a good mood?"

I wasn't sure how I felt about Ashton still worrying about Sawyer. I hadn't expected this when I'd planned to spend the summer there. It had been six months since the breakup. Normal people moved on after six months, didn't they? I mean, she was with Beau. Shouldn't everything be water under the bridge?

"He, uh, was fine." Okay, so that was a lie, but I wanted to protect him from her. He wouldn't want Ashton to know he was still affected by her and Beau.

She let out a sigh and plopped back down on the bed, folding her legs up underneath her and facing me. "Good. He and Beau kind of had some words at the field tonight. I had to jump in Beau's arms to keep them from tearing it up. That's why Sawyer left and ended up at Wings."

I hadn't seen them fight since we were kids. Surely, they weren't fighting over Ashton still. "What happened?" I asked, knowing I probably didn't want to hear it.

"Stupid stuff. Beau didn't like the way Sawyer spoke to me. It wasn't a big deal, but Beau got real upset and went on the defensive. They still haven't found a way to handle me being in the middle."

The last time I'd been sitting on her bed talking about the Vincent boys, I had told her that she needed to let both of them go. Even then I knew she wouldn't be able to. They were so much a part of her life. Beau, especially.

"Is Sawyer dating?" I asked, trying to sound as casual as possible.

Ashton let out a short laugh. "I wish."

That was odd. He was gorgeous, talented, athletic, polite, and funny—how did someone like him go six months without some girl managing to snag a date with him?

"Not even one date?"

Ashton shrugged and pulled her knees up to her chin, wrapping her arms around the front of her legs. "I think maybe one or two dates. Not sure. I don't ask, really. Sawyer still acts weird around me, and Beau gets very territorial if I bring up Sawyer. He doesn't like me talking about him much."

How sad for Sawyer. Ashton had been a big part of his life since they were twelve, but he couldn't really talk to her anymore without Beau standing near them. As much as I wanted Sawyer to be over Ashton, I didn't like the picture in my head. Sawyer, alone, bothered me. He didn't deserve that. He'd been so good to both of them.

"Welcome to the Jungle" started blaring, and Ashton reached for her cell phone.

"You cannot already be in bed," she purred into the phone. It had to be Beau. "Really? Oh, okay, well, that's good. I'm glad the two of you are out together." My ears perked up, and I studied my fingernails, trying to appear as if I weren't completely curious about the conversation.

"I love you, too. Be careful, and remember he doesn't drink much, so get him home safe." Was Sawyer drinking? With Beau?

Ashton smiled. "No, I love you more."

Oh, please.

"I'll keep it beside my pillow. Call me as soon as you get home." She lifted her eyes to smile brightly at me. "Yes, we're catching up. Okay, love you. Bye."

She dropped her phone into her lap and let out a happy sigh.

"I know you don't like how things went down and that Sawyer was hurt, but I love Beau so much, Lana. I'd do it all over again if I had to. I hated hurting Sawyer, I really did. I've never been so happy. Beau is wonderful." Her voice went all dreamy, and I fought the urge to roll my eyes.

Chapter 5

SAWYER

I still couldn't figure out why I was there. Sure, I'd been to Kayla's birthday parties every year since seventh grade, but that had been because Ash had wanted to go. This year what Ash wanted no longer mattered, so why the hell was I there?

Spill Canvas blared through the speakers outside. The pool had several different-colored strobe lights pointed at it from an upstairs balcony, making the water appear pink, purple, green, and yellow. Teak loungers surrounded the pool along with tiki torches. Last year Jake had bumped into one of those and an umbrella had caught on fire. Before it could get too out of hand, Beau had picked it up and chucked it into the pool. We'd laughed about that for weeks afterward.

I made my way over to the self-serve, makeshift bar right

outside the pool house, which basically consisted of large metal tubs filled with ice and drinks. If I was going to endure tonight, I needed alcohol. Lots of it.

"Sawyer!" Ryan Mason slurred. "The man has arrived." He was already drunk. That was no surprise. The Mason boys were the owners of the land where we had our field parties. Ryan's older brother had started the parties years back.

I nodded his way and reached for a bottle of Corona that was hidden under ice cubes.

"That's it, buddy. Drink up. Ain't got to impress the preacher's daughter anymore, do ya?" Ryan called out from the middle of the pool. He was lying on a float with some girl snuggled up beside him. I was pretty sure she had gone to our school.

I didn't respond to his asinine comment. Like Ash cared about that. Hell, she'd left me for Beau. Twisting off the top and throwing it into the recycle bin beside the drinks, I took a long swig of my beer. The cold liquid didn't make me feel better, but at least it tasted good.

Turning to walk back to the house and maybe find a television so I could turn on SportsCenter, I took only a few steps before the glass doors opened and out stepped Ashton, Beau, and Lana.

Ah hell, I should've stayed home. Ashton waved at Kayla and pulled Lana over to where Kayla was lounging with some of the other girls we'd graduated with. Beau's eyes met mine, and he sauntered over to stand beside me. Both his hands were tucked into the front pockets of his jeans.

"Didn't think you'd come to this," Beau said in way of greeting.

Shrugging, I held up the Corona in my hand. "Free beer."

Beau grinned and nodded. Free beer was definitely something he understood. His eyes didn't leave Ash as she chatted happily with the other girls. The tiny cover-up she was wearing over her bikini left little to the imagination. She'd never dressed like that when we'd dated. That probably had been another one of her attempts at being perfect for me. *What bullshit.*

"Better be Lana you're checking out," Beau warned.

I shifted my eyes to Lana and was surprised to see her in a pair of really tiny shorts. Her legs weren't tanned like Ash's, but they were long and shaped exactly like hers. The pale, creamy color was delicate-looking. I ran my gaze up her body and took in the way her hips flared just below a very small waist that was completely visible through the halter top she wore over her bikini. It was odd that she had so many freckles on her face. The rest of her body looked so perfectly smooth that she appeared almost airbrushed.

"I think she likes you." Beau's words broke into my thoughts. I tore my gaze off Lana's dark copper curls and looked at my brother.

"What?"

"Lana. She asked about you this evening. Wondered if you'd be here." Beau smirked. "I think she might have a crush on the quarterback."

I shifted my attention back to Lana at the same time she peered over her shoulder, and our eyes met. She froze, as if in shock I'd been looking her way. Ashton's cousin wasn't hard on the eyes and she was really sweet. I took another drink of my Corona as I played around with the idea of talking to Lana to get my mind off Ash.

"Told ya," Beau said in an amused tone.

Maybe he was right. Lana's mouth lifted in a small smile, and I remembered how soft her lips had felt under mine. It'd been one helluva kiss.

"Come on. Let's go get you something a little stronger than a beer. It's time you moved on from Ash before we end up beating the shit out of each other again."

Beau headed for the pool house and I followed my brother, reluctantly breaking the lingering gaze Lana and I had held longer than I'd expected.

LANA

Beau pressed his hand on the lower part of Ashton's back in a territorial way as he led her toward the stairs. I watched as she fought between the desire to go with her boyfriend and her duty to stay with me.

"I can't leave Lana," Ashton whispered.

Beau grabbed her waist and tugged her up against his chest. His eyes never once left her face. "Lana is a big girl and won't mind if I steal you away for a few minutes . . . or more." He lifted his hazel eyes and grinned at me. "You don't mind, do you, Lana?"

Like I was going to piss off Beau Vincent by admitting that I really didn't want to be left alone. Shaking my head, I forced a smile. "Um, no, that's fine. Y'all, uh, go do whatever."

Beau turned his gaze back to Ashton. "Please come with me." His voice had dropped, and his eyes became dark and pleading. No way Ashton was going to turn him down now.

"Okay," she whispered without giving me a second glance. I watched as Beau led her up the stairs. Surely, she wasn't going to have *sex* with him in Kayla's house. Shaking my head, I turned to head back outside. Maybe Sawyer would be alone, and I could work up the nerve to go talk to him.

Before I reached the door, Sawyer walked inside. His eyes seemed a little glassy and his normally perfectly styled hair was messy. I stopped and watched him as he scanned the room until his eyes found me and stopped. A slow grin spread across his lips, and he sauntered toward me. Was he staggering a little?

"Hey, Lana, what you doin' all alone?"

I swallowed the nervous knot in my throat as he stood so

close to me that my arm was touching his. "Uh, well, Ash and Beau went . . ." I pointed toward the stairs, unable to tell him what they'd gone to do.

His amused smile became an angry snarl as he shifted his focus to the steps, as if they were repugnant. Great, I'd gotten him all worked up over Beau and Ashton again.

A hand closed around mine, and I squeaked in surprise. Sawyer chuckled and slipped his warm fingers around my cold ones. "Come on, sweet little Lana. You can come entertain me since you've been left stranded. Besides, I've been looking at those long, sexy legs all night. You make them shorts look real good."

I gaped at him as he pulled me over to an empty couch. Had Sawyer just said my legs were sexy? I didn't have time to think about his statement before he was pulling me down to sit on his lap.

He buried his face in my hair and inhaled loudly. "Damn, you smell good," he murmured. One of his hands slipped around my waist and spread out across the front of my bare stomach while his other hand wrapped a strand of my hair around his finger.

"Feels like silk," he whispered, and ran my hair across his lips. After experiencing an initial shock, my heart started racing. This was the closest I'd ever gotten to a boy, and the fact it was Sawyer terrified and excited me all at once.

His nose trailed up my shoulder, and then he began nuzzling my neck. I couldn't help the shiver that ran through me when his warm breath tickled my ear. The hand on my stomach inched up a tiny bit, and he turned me around so that I was facing him.

"You feel real good, Lana. Makes me forget everything else," he murmured as his hand cupped the back of my head and gently guided my mouth to his.

The same intense hunger I'd felt the last time we'd kissed overtook me. His tongue darted out and licked at my bottom lip and he groaned. Sawyer Vincent *groaned* as he licked and tasted my mouth. I pressed closer to him and ran my hands through his dark locks, hoping this kiss didn't end as abruptly as the last one had.

When his tongue swept into my mouth, I was the one to groan. He tasted like something dark and dangerous. Cautiously I touched my tongue to his. Both his hands gripped my waist and picked me up to straddle him as he ran his hands up my back and pulled me tighter against his chest. His mouth left mine, and I started to protest until he began trailing kisses across my jawline and softly nipped my earlobe and kissed a trail down my neck. I wiggled anxiously as heat pooled in my belly and a strange tingling began to occur between my legs.

"Yo, Saw, get a room, man," a loud voice called out, breaking through my fogged brain. I stiffened, jerking out of the warmth of Sawyer's embrace. I'd completely forgotten that we were in the living room! Other people were around us. My face was on fire. I chanced a peek at Sawyer, who was watching me with an amused grin.

"Don't go getting all shy on me now, Lana," he drawled, squeezing my sides with his hands.

"Sawyer! What are you *doing*?" Ashton demanded from behind me, and I scrambled off his lap like I'd been doing something wrong.

"Well, Ash, I'm doin' exactly what it looks like I'm doin'," Sawyer replied.

"You were all over Lana!"

"Yeah, baby, I was. Your cousin is a sweet little thing. And she wasn't fighting me. I'm pretty damn sure she was enjoying herself too."

Hoots and whistles came from somewhere around us. I couldn't seem to do anything but stare at Sawyer in shock.

"She's off limits. Do you hear me? Don't you dare use her—"

"Use her? Really, Ash? You think that's what this was about? Because, baby, it ain't. I can be attracted to other girls. It *is* possible." The pleased tone in his voice was unmistakable. Why was he so pleased?

"That's not what I meant," Ashton all but yelled.

Sawyer raised his eyebrows in disbelief. "Really? 'Cause that's sure what it sounded and looked like from here, sweetheart."

"That's enough, Sawyer." Beau's voice startled me, and I turned to see him walking into the room. *Oh, good Lord,* he was mad.

"It ain't me this time, bro. She started it." Sawyer didn't sound worried at all about the fact that Beau looked ready to hurt someone.

"And if you don't shut your drunk-ass mouth, I'm going to end it." Beau's voice was cold and even.

Sawyer wasn't drunk, was he? I stared at him; he just looked relaxed. When my dad had come home drunk, he'd been loud and mean. Sawyer was sweet and gentle—or he had been before we'd been interrupted.

"Lana, just come on. We need to go," Ashton demanded from her spot beside Beau.

Sawyer's hand reached over and grabbed mine. "Don't leave," he said in a pleading whisper. That was all I needed. I'd come here for one reason: to get Sawyer Vincent to notice me. I wasn't about to leave when I had his attention.

"I want to stay here awhile longer, if that's okay," I replied, hoping Ashton didn't get angry. Not that she really had a reason to be.

"But he's—"

"Not your business," Sawyer said, interrupting Ashton.

Anger flared in Ashton's green eyes, and Beau pulled her tight against his side and whispered something to her. She seemed to relax a little, then nodded.

"Okay, fine. Stay. But do not let Sawyer drive you home. Beau and I'll come back and get you when you're ready. Just call."

I nodded. Sawyer hadn't promised to take me home anyway. That sounded like a good plan.

"Glad you two are leaving. Lana and I needed a room," Sawyer announced, standing up rather unsteadily and tugging me up beside him. Laughter from the audience we'd drawn was the wake-up call I needed.

Jerking my hand out of his grasp, I mentally cursed my fair skin and the blush I knew was covering my face and neck. Maybe Sawyer was drunk. I hoped he was, because insinuating to everyone around us that we were going to go do something in a bedroom was *not* something the Sawyer I knew would do.

"You know, I think I will leave with Ash and Beau," I replied, hoping I'd masked the humiliation in my voice.

"Wait. No. What'd I do?" Sawyer's hurt little boy voice almost stopped me. But his words, which had implied that we were going to go up to the bedroom and do God knows what while a room full of people listened, kept me moving toward Ashton.

"Come on," Ashton whispered, pulling me to her side and leading me out the door.

"Someone sober drive him home, or call me to come get him," Beau said in parting, before he turned and followed us outside.

"I'm not drunk!" Sawyer declared loudly.

Then the door closed, and I had to fight back the tears.

Chapter 6

SAWYER

I was drunk. I'd only been drunk one other time in my life, and that had been the day I'd found out about Beau and Ashton. I was almost positive that I was even drunker than I had been then. My stomach rolled, and I bent over for the third time and hurled into the bushes in the front of Kayla's yard. Cold sweat trickled down my face, and I rested my hands on my knees and closed my eyes, praying I didn't pass out in my own vomit. What the hell had I drunk? All I could remember was pouring some rum into a few or more of my Cokes. Maybe I'd stopped adding the Coke after a while and just went with straight rum. . . . No, wait, I'd switched to vodka. We'd run out of rum. My stomach heaved again, but there was nothing left to come out. Backing up, I leaned against the cold brick wall and let the fresh air cool me down.

"Drink this, you stupid fucker."

I peeled my eyes open to see Beau's annoyed expression as he pressed a chilled plastic bottle into my hand. Dropping my gaze, I saw he'd brought me water. The aftertaste of my regurgitated liquor wasn't appealing. I should have thanked him for coming to the rescue, but I just couldn't bring myself to do it.

Opening the bottle, I took a long swig and instantly felt better.

"Get a few more drinks, then come on. I'm taking you home."

His bossy attitude was beginning to get on my nerves. He wasn't suddenly the good brother—or cousin, as far as everyone else knew. Just because he had Ash didn't make him the smart one.

"Back off, Beau," I said with snarl, and took another drink of my water.

"I promised Ash I wouldn't knock some sense into you tonight. Don't make me break that promise."

Rolling my eyes, I pushed off from the side of the house where I'd been resting and walked past Beau toward my truck. I wasn't drunk anymore. I'd just expelled every drop of alcohol from my body in the Jenkinses' shrubbery.

"Don't do this, Sawyer. You've had too much to drink and you're ready to pass out. Let me take you home."

Stopping, I turned around and glared at him. "Why? All I do is piss off Ash. I can't stop looking at her. Wanting her. Why the fuck do you want to help me so bad?"

Beau let out a sigh and returned my glare. "Because you're my brother."

That was the crux of it all. It sure hadn't mattered to him that I was his brother when he'd taken my girl. Technically, he'd thought I was his cousin, but we'd always been as close as brothers.

"I thought we'd gotten our closure on this, Sawyer. You gave me your blessing. You gave Ash your blessing, and you walked away. What's wrong?"

What was wrong? Everything was wrong. He got my girl. He got the college I wanted to attend. He got every fucking damn thing I wanted in life.

"Nothing," I muttered, and turned around and headed for my truck again.

"Sawyer, I will literally force you into my truck if I have to." Beau didn't sound angry, just sincere.

Tonight I wasn't up to handling a one-on-one with him. I was more than positive I'd lose and possibly have a few bruises to show for it.

"Fine. Drive me home."

After Beau dropped me off, I'd taken a long hot shower and then crawled into bed. Luckily, neither of my parents got up to check on me. Once I pulled the sheets up over my waist, I stared at the ceiling and replayed the fit Ashton had pitched tonight in my head. She'd been angry. Why? Because I'd been making out with Lana in public? All we'd done was kiss. Granted, it was one really hot kiss, and that girl's skin was incredible to touch. Her hair smelled like some sort of soft flower, and before we'd been interrupted by a stupid demand that we get a room, I'd been thinking about how I wanted to taste the skin in the curve of her neck. Her pulse had been racing under my lips and it had been intoxicating . . . like nothing I'd ever experienced before.

Ashton had put a quick stop to things, though. She'd been spitting mad—almost a little too mad. Was she . . . jealous? Could she be? I hadn't really dated anyone since our breakup. She'd never seen me with any girls—certainly not making out like that. But . . . jealous . . . maybe. A small smile tugged at the corner of my mouth, and I reached for my cell phone.

Me: Please tell Lana I'm sorry I got drunk and was a jerk.

I pressed send and waited to see what Ashton's reply was. Almost immediately my phone dinged. Grinning, I sat up and read.

Ashton: Yes, you were. I'll tell her. Just stay away from her, Sawyer.

She *was* jealous. She didn't like me being interested in someone else. Ashton wanted both Vincent brothers enthralled with her. Well, this could turn out to be fun as hell.

Me: Can't do that, Ash. I really like her.

I almost thought she wasn't going to reply when the phone lit up and I read her text.

Ashton: I don't want her to get hurt.

I laughed to myself; I knew better. She didn't want to share my affection. Stingy little brat.

Me: I wouldn't hurt her. I want to spend some
time with her. Can I have her number?
Ashton: Not tonight.

I lay back in bed, grinning, thinking that Ash had just made this game too fun to walk away.

LANA

"Lana?" Ashton's voice broke into my internal battle of staying there or just giving up and going back home.

"Yeah," I replied, wishing I could successfully fake-sleep.

Ashton opened the door to the guest bedroom where my aunt had insisted I sleep, instead of the extra mattress on the floor of Ashton's room where I'd normally slept. I sat up and watched as she walked over to me, wringing her hands. That one small nervous mannerism of hers told me that this was about Sawyer. Not something I wanted to talk about—at least not tonight.

"Um . . . do you, uh, do you like Sawyer?"

How blind could one person be? Ashton had always been clueless to the world around her. She had her small bubble, and she worried about what affected her and nothing more. I was invading her bubble, and she was noticing things that she should have picked up on years ago.

"Yes, a little."

Her bare, perfectly tanned shoulders lifted with a sigh, and she nodded. "I thought so."

She sat down cautiously on the edge of the bed. I studied her face and wondered if the concern was for me or herself or possibly Sawyer.

"Sawyer wasn't himself tonight. You know that." She lifted her eyes to meet mine, and I saw only sadness—no jealousy or anxiety. She was just sad.

"I know. I didn't even realize he drank. I thought that was Beau's M.O."

"He normally doesn't. Tonight I saw a side of Sawyer I'd

never seen before. He was very . . . Beau-like. Or at least the way Beau used to be."

Her words made everything click. The puzzle that Sawyer had created tonight all fell into place. He had acted like Beau back when Beau wanted Ashton and didn't have her. A small ache in my chest started and, unfortunately, it was all too familiar. It was the same ache I'd felt when I'd seen the tender, completely devoted look Sawyer bestowed on Ashton every time he glanced her way, which had been often.

"Makes sense," I muttered, more to myself than to Ashton.

Instead of asking me what I meant, she only nodded and stared helplessly at the pale blue wall across from her. At least she got it, and I didn't have to spell it out for her. Sawyer was coping with not having Ashton by drinking and acting out. It had been six months for crying out loud. How long did he need?

"He texted me tonight."

"Who?" I assumed she was talking about Sawyer, but with Ashton you never could be sure which Vincent boy she was talking about.

"Sawyer. He asked about you. Wanted me to tell you he was sorry."

My stupid heart sped up, and I tried to keep my face composed. I reminded myself he'd probably been more worried about Ashton's feelings than mine.

"Oh" was the only response I could muster.

"I don't know what his motives are, Lana. I mean, you are gorgeous and he is a guy. I can see that he could be interested in you—"

"But you're also worried he's using me to get to you." I finished her thought for her.

Ashton pulled her bottom lip between her teeth and grimaced. Yep, it sounded bad when said out loud. But it was the truth.

"The Sawyer I know, the Sawyer I loved isn't calculating and cruel. But the Sawyer I knew also would have never gotten drunk at a party and made out with a girl in public. Heck, I'm pretty sure you did more with Sawyer on that couch than I did with Sawyer during the three years we dated." Ashton let out a hard, short laugh. "I basically had to beg him to do more than a few chaste kisses. He was so controlled. Tonight, when I came downstairs and saw the two of you, and well, his hands. . ." she trailed off.

I knew exactly where his hands had been and remembering made my face heat up.

"I guess what I'm trying to say is, be careful. I don't know what he's up to, and I don't want to believe he is trying to get to me through you. I just don't think he would do that. Honestly, if you and Sawyer became an item, I'd be happy for both of you. He's a wonderful guy. He just wasn't 'my guy' . . . ya know?"

I didn't know what to say to her. I was surprised she was so okay with Sawyer moving on. Sure, Beau was a hottie, but if Sawyer had been mine, I'd be devastated to see him move on.

"He wants your cell phone number. I didn't give it to him. I wasn't sure what you wanted me to do."

"Give it to him," I replied quickly.

Ashton laughed and nodded before standing up. "Well, okay, then. Glad to know where you stand." The teasing in her voice was a relief. She really was okay with this.

"This summer . . . my coming here . . . It wasn't just about wanting to spend time with you before we go off to college."

Ashton grinned and raised her eyebrows. "I can't believe you're telling me a Vincent boy—not me—brought you to Grove, Alabama."

Shrugging, I returned her smile. "They're hard to resist."

"Don't I know it?"

I stood at the window and watched as Ashton jumped in Beau's arms and proceeded to kiss his face all over as if she hadn't just seen him last night. It was kind of gross. He was shirtless and covered in sweat. He reached up and turned his dirty University of Alabama baseball hat around backward before grabbing Ashton's face and taking over her wandering lips. Shaking my head, I turned away from the major public display of affection those two were sharing with the entire street. She'd been clean when she left, and now she had Beau Vincent sweat—not to mention the grass probably stuck to his body—all over her outfit. She'd better hope her daddy didn't decide to come home for an early lunch. That would *not* go over well.

The short clip of "Tell Him" by Colbie Caillat alerted me that I had a text message. Running over to the dresser, I grabbed the phone; my heart fluttered before I even read the message.

Sawyer: It's Sawyer. I'm sorry about last night. Let me make it up to you. I'm taking the boat out today. Come with me, please.

I didn't even give myself time to think it through. I quickly typed.

Me: Okay. When?

Playing hard to get might be the best way to handle this if Sawyer actually liked me. But I wasn't sure. If I was just a weapon to use against Ashton, then I needed to change that. I needed to make him see me.

Sawyer: Can you be ready in an hour?

Me: Yes.

Sawyer: Wear a swimsuit. Preferably that bikini you had on last night.

I had to take a deep calming breath, and I reread his request several times before typing.

Me: K.

Chapter 7

SAWYER

Lana opened the front door the moment I pulled into Ash's driveway. I needed to fix the mess I'd made last night, so instead of enjoying the view of her long, creamy legs showcased in tiny, red shorts, I jumped out of the truck and walked around the front of the cab so I could open the door and help her get in.

A shy smile played on her full lips as I met her on the other side of my truck. Yep, I had hope. Even after the stunt I'd pulled last night, she was still affected by me. Guilt settled in my stomach when I stared into her trusting eyes.

"Hey." Her Georgia drawl wasn't bad either. I'd never realized Lana had a sexy voice.

"I'm glad you've forgiven me enough to come today."

She shrugged. Her shoulders were dainty, and a few freckles graced the smooth skin she was exposing with a sleeveless top. I hadn't noticed those last night, and the urge to kiss each one shocked me.

"Not much to forgive. You acted like an ass, but you were drunk. I should've been paying closer attention."

I couldn't keep from laughing. Lana McDaniel had just called me an ass.

"That's awfully considerate of you," I replied.

"Hmmm . . . maybe so."

I opened the truck door and reached out to take her hand as she stepped up into the cab. The shorts rode even farther up her legs and, through my appreciative gaze, I noticed one lone freckle incredibly close to the curve of her heart-shaped bottom. My pulse sped up, and I forced myself to stop ogling her backside.

Unsure about whether or not my voice was going to betray me, I didn't say anything as I closed the door and went back around to the driver's side.

Once we headed toward the boat launch, I glanced over at Lana. "You still know how to wakeboard, don't you?" I'd spent hours teaching her how to board one summer when we were in middle school while Ash and Beau heckled her from the boat.

A small smile tugged on her lips, and I wondered if she was

remembering that day too. It had been us against Ash and Beau. For once I'd felt like I had a team. It was always me trying to rein in those two, but that day I'd had a partner. Granted, I'd wanted Ash as my partner. That was the summer before everything changed, the summer before I became quarterback and I got Ash.

"Yes, I think. Isn't it like a bicycle? Ya know, once you learn you never forget?"

The guys were going to enjoy this a little too much. If I hadn't needed a spotter and a backup driver, we would be doing this alone today. But skiing and boarding, with only two people, wasn't safe. Someone needed to be watching the rider and, if I wanted to wakeboard, and I did—especially with Lana—then I needed another driver.

"Hmmm . . . maybe a little. It might take you a few tries if you're rusty," I finally replied.

Lana let out a small groan, and I bit back a laugh. She'd had the hardest time learning to get up on skis, and then the wakeboard had almost done her in. I always admired her determination, though. She hadn't given up.

"If we are skiing and wakeboarding, others will be there, right?"

I nodded, noticing the small disappointment in her voice. She wanted me alone. I liked that—a lot.

"Will Ethan be there?"

My small moment of pleasure evaporated.

"Ethan? Uh, probably." *Well, shit.* I had forgotten about their little bonding episode at Wings. Ethan hadn't been at the party last night. He didn't know about our public display of affection. No, wait—he probably did. That was gossip worthy. Someone was bound to have told him by now.

"Oh, good. I'll at least have one other friend there."

Hell, *no.* I'd have to pull Ethan aside without her noticing and make sure he understood Lana was off-limits.

Again the guilt started tugging at me and I pushed it away. Sure, Ethan might be more sincere about his interest in Lana, but she was here only for the summer. Then we were all heading off to college. If anyone was going to have a summer fling with her, it was going to be me. End of story. No reason for guilt. This was a means to an end. Besides, I took a quick peek over at Lana; it wasn't like I didn't enjoy her company. She was gorgeous, smart, and funny. Plus, being with her was going to drive Ashton mad, maybe even send her running right back to my arms. . . . There was that damn guilt again. I needed a beer. That always helped wash away my conscience.

LANA

My cell phone rang, and I quickly pulled it out of my pocket. It was Ashton. I'd texted her that I was going boating with

Sawyer today. She must have thought that warranted a phone call instead of a text reply.

"Hey," I said, trying hard not to look at Sawyer. He was driving, but I could feel his eyes on me.

"Are you two going alone? Because if you are, that isn't safe. Beau and I can come too."

No way did I want Ashton anywhere near Sawyer today. I needed to get his attention, and when Ashton was around, he was single-minded. "No, we're going skiing. Others are coming too. It'll be safe."

"If that's Ash, tell her that she and Beau are welcome to join us," Sawyer piped up. Dang it.

"Tell him thanks, but if y'all have other people going, it'll probably be more fun without Beau and Sawyer and me all together. . . ." She trailed off.

"Okay, I'll tell him."

"Tonight Beau and I are going to go to the beach to eat some crab claws, then go hear Little Big Town play at the Wharf. Ethan also has two tickets and was wondering if you'd like to go, ya know . . . with him."

Ethan? I turned my head so I could peek at Sawyer. He was watching the road, but I could tell his attention was completely focused on my conversation with Ashton. Annoyed with the reasons behind his interest, I decided two could play this game.

"Sure, I'd love to go tonight. I'm about to see Ethan, so I'll tell him myself."

Sawyer's head whipped around to stare at me, and I flashed him an innocent smile and said my good-byes to Ashton before hanging up.

"Ashton and Beau have other plans for the day. She said to tell you thanks, though." If he wanted to know about Ethan, he was going to have to *ask*.

"What did she want you to tell Ethan?"

I opened my mouth to respond almost automatically but snapped it shut quickly. That wasn't his business. Just because he asked me didn't mean I had to tell him. The old Lana would have blurted out whatever he wanted to know. The new Lana didn't do that. The new Lana wasn't a love-struck puppy. . . . Okay, maybe I was, but he didn't have to know that.

"If I'd have wanted you to know the details of my conversation, I'd have put Ashton on speakerphone," I finally replied.

"Ouch. I was just asking."

Maybe I'd gone a little overboard with my snarky comment. I did want Sawyer to like me, and he had invited me to go out skiing with him.

"Sorry. It was just nothing of your concern. I didn't mean to sound so snappy."

Sawyer didn't respond and silence engulfed the truck.

*   *   *

Once Sawyer pulled into the parking lot at the boat launch, I'd had enough time to decide how to handle his silence. Spending the day on a boat with an annoyed Sawyer didn't sound like fun.

"I really am sorry I was so rude. It was nothing, really."

Sawyer turned the engine off and turned to meet my gaze. He studied me a moment, then finally nodded. "Okay. I shouldn't have stuck my nose in your business. I just thought we were friends. I didn't really think about it when I asked."

Great. I felt as low as the dirt on the bottom of my shoes.

"We are friends. I don't know why I snapped at you like that. I guess I was embarrassed about the topic." Which was partially true.

A frown puckered his brow, which was ridiculously hot. "Why would Ash ask you to tell Ethan something embarrassing?"

Perfect. I'd backed myself against a wall. I couldn't exactly shut him out again. I didn't like having him go all surly and quiet on me. The best course of action would be to lie.

"I've never been on a date before. Ethan asked me to go with him to a concert tonight. Or he asked Ashton to ask me if I'd go with him." *Or* I could just blurt out the whole truth and look like an idiot. Dang it! I needed to work on my lying skills. I had none. I'd opened my mouth to lie and out came the truth instead. I forced myself not to grimace, and reached for the door handle. The complete surprise in Sawyer's eyes was humiliating. I was eighteen years old and I had never been on a date. It was sad. And now Sawyer knew just how pathetic I was.

"Wait." Sawyer's hand shot out and grabbed my arm to stop me before I jumped down out of the truck.

Sighing, I turned back around to look into his sympathetic, astonished eyes but found that they weren't exactly full of sympathy or astonishment. Instead he looked . . . frustrated.

Well, that's interesting.

"Do you like Ethan?"

Yes, I liked Ethan. He was nice, thoughtful, funny, sweet, and he was attracted to me. There was no ex-girlfriend he was hung up on standing in my way. But he wasn't Sawyer.

Nodding, I didn't say any more. Instead I waited.

Sawyer opened his mouth to say something, then shut it and closed his eyes tightly before shaking his head and letting go of my arm. "Never mind. Come on. Let's go."

He opened his door and stepped out. I'd have given anything to get him to say what it was he had stopped himself from saying just then. But the conversation was over. His curiosity had been cured, and I had an entire day to dwell on the fact that I may have just killed any chance I had with him. Ethan was his friend, and after the mess with Beau, I doubted Sawyer would ever make a move on a girl that had dated his friend first.

Chapter 8

SAWYER

If Ethan whispered in her ear one more time, I was going to throw his ass off the damn boat. The only reason he'd managed to stay on it this long was because Lana didn't look all that happy about his attempt at flirting. She wasn't laughing and smiling at him like she had been at the restaurant. Instead she appeared a little uptight about something. Had she decided in the light of day that Ethan wasn't all that interesting? God, I hoped so. I didn't want her for the right reasons, and that was making it very hard to be selfish and calculating. Lana was so freaking sweet, and in no way did I want to hurt her. If Ethan made her happy, I wasn't sure I could stand in the way just to get Ash all worked up.

"Should I warn E. to step back?" Jake's voice broke into my

thoughts, and I jerked my gaze off Lana and Ethan to focus on driving the boat.

"From what?" I asked in a bored voice.

Jake let out a snort. "From the murderous glare you're shooting his way."

Since when did Jake decide to start paying attention to the world around him? Shaking my head, I turned back and checked on Kayla and Toby. They'd been out there trying to outdo each other for more than twenty minutes. If I didn't make a sharp unexpected turn, they'd both stay up for another twenty minutes. I needed a distraction.

"Hold on, I'm about to sling them!" I called out loudly. My eyes immediately found Lana, and she had a tight grip on the side of the boat as she watched Kayla and Toby, frowning.

Jerking the wheel hard to the left sent Kayla and Toby flying through the air. I could hear Kayla squeal and Toby yell out something very close to "Motherfu—" before they hit the water with a loud slap.

"Oh my god! Are they okay?" Lana asked, gaping back at me with a horrified expression. They were fine. I knew the correct way and place to sling someone off their wakeboard. We'd all been doing this since we were kids. Those two knew how to safely land after a good slinging.

I pointed at the water where Kayla and Toby had landed. Lana spun back around in her seat to see that they had both resurfaced and were fine. Kayla was holding her board, and Toby was kissing her as she giggled loudly.

I saw Lana's shoulders relax.

"That's the way Saw likes to tell someone their time is up," Ethan said, smiling at her with a ridiculous googly-eyed expression on his face. I would be doing the boy a favor taking her away from him. He was making an ass of himself.

Lana turned to look back at me with those big green eyes. I had to swallow hard; her eyes were so much like Ashton's. "I don't think I want a turn."

Chuckling, I nudged Jake. "Take it."

"I'm not going to drive you. I'm going to go out there with you," I informed her.

Lana shifted her fearful gaze from me to Jake, who was now at the wheel. She didn't trust him any more than she did me.

"Um, I don't know. Maybe . . . Maybe Ethan could drive," she suggested.

The frustrated frown he was wearing because I was the one about to go out with Lana was replaced with a pleased grin. She trusted him and he liked it—of course he did.

"Whatever," Jake said, grabbing his drink and plopping back down on the bench where he'd been sprawled out before I'd given him the wheel.

Ethan went over, took the wheel, and cut the engine so that Toby and Kayla could climb back on.

I reached over and grabbed the wakeboard Toby was handing me. "You could've just motioned for us to let go," Toby said with a grumble as he reached for Kayla and helped her crawl up on the dive board.

"But that was so much more fun to watch," I replied, taking Kayla's life vest and handing it to Lana. "This one is the only one that'll fit you. The rest are all too big."

Lana took it and shivered as the cold water dripped off the jacket and onto her warm skin.

"Actually, that's not true. He has a much better one tucked away under the seats, but it's Ash's. He gave it to her for her birthday one year, along with the better wakeboard—at least for girls. But he won't let anyone else use it, even though—"

"Don't, babe," Toby interrupted as he gently pushed Kayla toward the back of the boat.

I couldn't bring myself to look back at Lana. I'd really rather she didn't know about Ash's stuff. I did still have vest tucked away under the bench seat. I wasn't ready to let someone else use it. Seeing someone else put it on would be another door closed. This had been something Ash and I did together. And she'd been so excited when I got her the new board. We'd even lain out on the water and floated on it that night while she rained kisses over my face and told me how wonderful I was—back when she'd still been mine.

"Here's your vest," Jake called out as he threw my nice dry

life vest at me. Catching it as it slammed into my chest, I quickly put it on and threw my board out onto the water.

"Sorry, I'm rusty. Do I just jump in?" Lana asked from the dive board, staring down at me with a worried frown.

I swam over to her. "Sit down," I said. She did so quickly, not taking her eyes off me. I reached for her waist and eased her into the water.

"Eeeep, it's cold!" she squealed, and her hands squeezed my arms tightly. Her full bottom lip quivered a little, and I couldn't stop myself from kissing her. I'd made her wear a cold, wet life vest because I was too much of a baby to pull out Ashton's. The least I could do was warm her lips up.

She tensed, but only briefly, the moment my mouth touched hers. Both her hands slid slowly up my arms and into my hair as I held her waist and pulled her closer to me. Pressing small innocent kisses on the corner of her mouth only whetted my appetite. I took a small taste of her bottom lip, and when her mouth opened in a small gasp, I plunged ahead. I needed to feel the soft pressure of her lips against mine. I tangled my tongue with hers as she pressed against me, running her hands through my wet locks. Yeah, that was good. That was real good. Sliding my hand down her hip, I pulled a leg up to wrap around my waist. A soft little moan escaped her as the *V* between her legs opened and pressed against the proof that I was enjoying this just a little too much. Ah, hell, that was better than good.

"Could you stop mauling her in public?" Jake's annoyed tone reminded me that we had a boat full of people behind us getting an up-close view. I pulled back, and the small, frustrated groan from Lana had me thinking I didn't really give a damn who saw us. But her eyes focused, and she glanced over my shoulder to see our curious audience.

Her cheeks turned bright pink as she ducked her head. Curled tendrils of her hair had gotten loose from the sloppy bun she'd put her hair in once we'd gotten on the boat. She swallowed nervously, her throat muscles moving behind the smooth, pale skin of her neck.

"I wanna kiss that spot . . . right there," I murmured as I ran the pad of my thumb over the place where her pulse beat heavily. It was as sexy as it was delicate.

"Oh," she replied breathlessly.

"Are you gonna board or not?" Toby called from behind us. I scowled at the nosy bunch of people I'd brought with us.

His question didn't warrant a reply. I reached for the board he'd thrown and moved it beside Lana. "You remember how this works?"

Taking a deep breath, Lana nodded and unwrapped her legs from my waist, eliciting a growl from me. I'd been enjoying the forbidden warmth.

The flicker of surprise in her eyes made it very hard for me not to pull her back.

"Yeah, I think so," she replied.

I turned to grab my board and lifted my eyes to see Ethan glaring at me. I gave him an apologetic shrug and headed out to make sure Lana was strapped on to the board correctly before Ethan started up the boat.

"He looks angry," Lana said, studying Ethan as I swam over to check her position.

"Yeah, he does."

"Do you think he'll sling us?"

I shook my head. Ethan was pissed, but he wasn't stupid. Lana had trusted him. He wouldn't screw that up. Also, I'd beat the shit out of him if he scared her. I was pretty sure he knew that, too.

"Is the fit tight? You feel locked in?"

She nodded and gave me a nervous smile.

LANA

What the heck had just happened? My body was still tingling, and I couldn't even think about the strange sensations going on in my um . . . private area. *Dear God, I'd been about to hump Sawyer right there in the water in front of everyone.*

"You ready?" Sawyer asked from beside me. I nodded and hoped that I was. It had been a while, but I knew how it felt when I was pulling back on the rope just the right amount.

The motor on the boat roared to life, and Ethan gunned

it, which I'd also been expecting. When Kayla and Toby had gone first, I had been sure to pay attention to everything they did. Kayla jumping the wake and flying up in the air wasn't something I was going to give a go, but I had still watched carefully.

Once I was safely up and not about to pitch forward into the water, I chanced a peek at Sawyer. He was grinning at me with approval, and my chest tightened. He was so beautiful. He closed the space between us, and I focused on not losing my balance, reminding myself he knew what he was doing. I just needed to focus on not moving to the left or right.

"You got this." Sawyer smiled at me, and then he was gone. I watched as he swung out, jumping the wake and flying even higher in the air than Kayla had done before coming back down, and he grinned like a little boy as the group on the boat whooped and hollered. I didn't even swing out to the right; I had no doubt I'd wipe out if I gave it a go. I took quick peeks over at Sawyer as he continued to do tricks on his side of the boat.

My arms were burning, and holding on was becoming increasingly harder. Biting down on my bottom lip, I tried to deal with the pain.

"Your arms burning?" Sawyer called out as he pulled in beside me.

I nodded, hating to end his fun.

"Let go of the rope on three," he replied, and began counting.

We both let go of our ropes when he said three, then sank down slowly into the water.

"Take your board off!" Sawyer called out as he stayed in position. He was going to go again without me. I didn't feel as bad for needing to stop.

The boat got back to us about the time I had unstrapped the board from my feet.

"Give Toby the board, then come here," Sawyer instructed, and I did as I was told. Maybe he needed help with something.

"You going again?" Jake yelled from his spot on the boat.

Sawyer nodded. "Yep, her arms were burning."

Toby took the board from my hands, and once he had it safely on the boat, I swam over to Sawyer.

"Sit in my lap and straddle me. Wrap your legs around my waist and hold on real tight," Sawyer said with a wicked grin in his eyes.

"What? W-why?" I stuttered, confused.

He let go of the rope with one hand and motioned me to come closer. "Come on, Lana. Wrap those long legs around my waist. I won't let you get hurt. Trust me."

A squeal and clapping distracted me, and I turned to look back at the boat. Kayla was extremely pleased.

"Do it, Lana! I've seen Sawyer do this with Ash many times!" Kayla called out.

I turned back to Sawyer. "But Ash can do tricks. I can't."

"All you have to do is hold on tight to me. Wrap your legs and arms around me, and I got the rest of this."

Excitement and fear battled each other as I gave in, slipping my legs around his waist and wrapping my arms around his neck.

"Hmmm . . . that's nice," Sawyer whispered into the curve of my neck. My heart began racing for a completely different reason when the boat fired up. I tightened my hold on him and buried my face in his shoulder. A warm, sexy chuckle vibrated within his chest.

We were up and going before I could think about anything else. My legs clamped down on his waist so tightly the hard arousal I'd felt earlier was firmly pressed against me.

"Ah, hell," he whispered in my ear, and I shifted, wondering if I weighed too much or was holding on too tight.

"Please, Lana, don't move. I can't concentrate when you do that."

I sucked in a breath and pulled back to peer up at him.

The smoldering gleam in his eyes sent my body into a warm frenzy.

"Am I hurting you?" I managed to croak out.

Sawyer shook his head and pressed a kiss to my forehead. "Not the way you think. Hang on. I'm going to give you a little bit of a ride."

I pressed back up against him and forced myself to keep my eyes open as he swung out to the left. The moment we went airborne, I gasped in delight. It was so freeing. Then we were back on the water with such ease that it wasn't frightening at all.

"You like that?" he asked, his mouth close to my ear so he didn't have to yell.

"That was fun," I assured him.

"Good, 'cause we're going higher this time," he replied, and we were flying out to the right and in the air so quickly that my stomach fluttered wildly.

"Oh wow," I said breathlessly as he landed the board.

"It's awesome, isn't it?"

Then we were slowing down and sinking into the water.

"Thank you for trusting me," he said as we settled down in the water to wait for the boat to come back and get us.

"Thank you for the ride."

Chapter 9

SAWYER

As soon as Lana closed the door to Ashton's house, I pulled my phone out of my pocket and dialed Beau.

"Yeah," he answered, on the third ring.

"I need a ticket to that concert tonight. I'm coming with you."

Beau didn't respond right away, but then he let out a sigh. "Little Miss Lana is gettin' to ya, huh?"

The memory of how she felt wrapped around my waist flooded me, and I swallowed hard. "Yeah, she is."

"Ash hooked her up with E. tonight. You know this, right?"

My blood boiled. Yes, I knew it, but I was going to stop it. Ethan wanted Lana only for the summer. He was headed to UT in the fall, and Lana was headed . . . Well, I didn't know where Lana was headed, but she was going off to college too. Yes, I wanted to make Ash jealous, but the idea of spending time with Lana was growing more and more appealing for no other reason than she made me forget. When I was with her, I wasn't thinking about Ashton.

"She was with *me* today. You owe me, Beau. A helluva lot. I need to be there tonight."

"Ash is gonna be pissed. She doesn't trust your motives, and I'm not real sure I do either."

"You've seen Lana. What's there not to like? Why would I want her for any other reason than she's hot as hell and available this summer? I need the distraction. I think it'll be good for all of us."

Beau was silent for a moment "The concert is sold out, but Ash got Leann two tickets, and she's driving over from the beach to go with us. Her date just bailed on her, and she's looking for someone to take with her. She might not want to give you the ticket as her date, but I'm pretty sure she'd sell it to you."

"I still got her number. I'll call her. Thanks." I didn't wait for him to reply before I hung up and scrolled through my contacts for Leann's name.

Ashton had initially asked us all to drive separate vehicles since Beau and I drove trucks and Ethan drove a Jeep. I didn't like that plan because it put me alone with Leann, and Lana alone with Ethan. Not the combination I was going for. So I borrowed Mom's Mercedes crossover. No one could argue that this wasn't a better idea—except maybe Ethan, who hadn't been in on the details. I'd handled it with Beau, who, in return, got Ashton to agree.

I'd started to ask Beau to take the backseat so Lana and Ethan would be closer to me, but the idea of Beau tucked away from everyone with Ashton made my chest ache. I didn't think I could handle it. So I remained quiet as Ethan quickly took the back row, holding Lana's hand as she stepped into the car. The ache from thinking about Ash and Beau was instantly extinguished by red-hot jealousy. Ethan's eyes were taking in Lana's cute little bottom; she'd barely covered up in that sundress.

"I think you just growled," Leann whispered as she stepped past me and opened the passenger door. Jerking my gaze off Ethan as he moved in beside Lana, I went to get in. This was going to be one long-ass thirty-minute drive.

"Still scowling," Leann teased from beside me. I shot her a glare that only caused her to giggle. "I really thought you'd never get over Ash. I'm surprised," she said under her breath, then pulled down the mirror in front of her to peek back at Lana and Ethan.

"If it helps, I don't think she's that into him," she said and then flipped the visor back up.

"Find whatever you want to listen to" was my only response to her nosy comments.

Leann clicked her tongue, grinning before leaning forward and scanning the channels.

"You know, Ethan is a good guy. He doesn't have any ulterior motives."

Grinding my teeth, I shook my head and shot her a warning glance.

"You used to be such a polite, nice guy, Sawyer Vincent. You've changed—a lot."

I adjusted the rearview mirror so that Lana was directly in my sight. She was watching me. The angry frustration melted away when she gave me a shy smile. Winking, I glanced back at the road and decided the car would be the only place Ethan got her away from me. He sure as hell better enjoy himself.

"Is that Ash or Lana you're checking up on?" Leann asked.

I realized I'd forgot about Ashton. My stomach knotted up. What was happening? Ash was right behind me, sitting next to Beau. I reached up and adjusted the mirror just in time to see Ash laugh and lay her head on Beau's shoulder. The familiar ache returned. Her eyes lifted and met mine. The laughter that had been sparkling in them vanished, and a concerned sadness came over her face. I missed those eyes laughing up at me. Gripping the steering wheel harder, I focused my attention on the road instead of the girl who I'd always love and the girl who sent me into a lustful fog every time she got close.

"You might wanna adjust that mirror." Beau's low warning came from behind me. If only I could hate him. Because, I wanted to. So badly.

Reaching up, I fixed the mirror so I couldn't see either girl, and I turned up the song Leann had chosen: "Break Your Little Heart" by All Time Low. It was fitting.

LANA

"I'm glad you came with me tonight," Ethan said, leaning into me a little.

I tore my eyes off the back of Sawyer's head. "Thank you for asking me," I replied, hoping the disappointment in my voice wasn't obvious. When Ashton told me that Sawyer had bought Leann's extra ticket and arranged for us all to ride together, I'd hoped it had been because of me, not her. Then he'd gotten in the car and fixed his rearview mirror so he could see me, and my heart had done a silly little flip. But within seconds he'd adjusted it so he could see Ashton instead. He hadn't been looking at me when he winked. . . . He'd been looking at Ashton. Beau had noticed too.

Ethan glanced back up at Sawyer and sighed. "Not sure why he's doing this," he whispered. "Sorry, but it looks like we're going to have to witness more of the Vincent boys' drama tonight. Sawyer isn't ever going to be able to let Ashton go, even though she's obviously let him go."

The nausea that followed his words wasn't surprising. I'd

been thinking the same thing, but hearing it from someone else was hard. I was so sure Sawyer had seen *me* today. I could feel his attraction to me. But then what did I know about guys and sex? I knew nothing. If any guy had his crotch pressed between a girl's legs, he'd probably get hard. From what I'd heard about guys, they couldn't help it.

Sighing, I slunk back in my seat and crossed my legs. My hope that tonight was about me was now gone. Ethan deserved more than me being hung up on getting Sawyer's attention. After all, Ethan, not Sawyer, was the one paying for my meal and my ticket.

"I've never been to a concert before," I told him, wanting to change the subject.

Ethan's eyes lit up. "Really? So I'm your first," he said, wagging his eyebrows teasingly. I couldn't help but laugh.

"I guess you are," I replied in the flirty tone I'd practiced at home alone in my room but had never used on an actual guy.

His eyes widened for a second, then he closed the small distance between us and slid his hand over my thigh to take my hand in his. And I let him. Because really, why shouldn't I?

Once we arrived at the beachside restaurant, I'd had time to get over my disappointment enough to enjoy myself—somewhat. If I had to watch Sawyer moon over Ashton all night, I might end up in the bathroom with the need to hurl again. Right then, however, I was good.

"You'll love this place. They have the best fried oyster po' boys," Ethan informed me as we made our way toward the steps that led up to the restaurant.

"Or you could eat them raw." Sawyer's voice was so close to my ear that it startled me. Jerking my attention off our destination, I turned to look at Sawyer, who had fallen into step beside me. He shot me a sexy little grin. "I'll share my dozen with you."

"Dozen?" I asked, still dazzled by the tantalizing smell of his cologne and the brush of his fingers as he lightly grazed mine.

"Raw oysters," he replied in a lazy drawl.

"Oh, I've never eaten one before. Not sure I want to." My voice sounded breathless and affected by him. I was just weak where Sawyer was concerned.

"I'll teach you exactly how to do it so it goes down nice and smooth." His voice had dropped and gone husky. I wanted to fan myself, because suddenly it was very, very hot out there. The sea breeze did nothing to cool me off.

"Oh" was all I could manage as a reply.

"If she wants oysters, I'll get them for her," Ethan replied in an annoyed tone, reminding me that he was on my other side.

"I was just offering to share, E. No need to get testy," Sawyer replied, not taking his eyes off me. His fingers softly tangled with mine then traced a caress up the inside of my arm. I had to clench my teeth to keep from making an embarrassing sound caused by the addicting feel of his touch.

Ethan opened the door and pulled me over closer to him, then placed his hand on my lower back to direct me inside the restaurant. He was putting himself between me and Sawyer, which only made me feel guilty. I'd all but melted into a puddle at Sawyer's feet while on a date with Ethan.

"I've got to go to the little girl's room. Come with me, Lana," Leann said as she grabbed my arm and led me back to the restroom and away from the rest of the group.

The moment the door closed behind me, Leann spun around. "Whoa, girl. Do you need me to splash some cold water on your face? After witnessing that I think *I* may need to cool off."

Letting out a moan, I covered my face with my hands. *Great, everyone had noticed.* Why did Sawyer do this to me? I was at his beck and call. It was ridiculous. He was using me to make Ashton jealous, and I was falling right into his arms. *Ugh!*

"I'm sorry," I finally said, my hands covering my mouth.

Leann chuckled. "Sorry for what? You haven't done anything. Sawyer Vincent is hot, Lana. He has never, and I mean never, unleashed what I just witnessed on anyone ever. Not even Ashton. I can't believe I just saw him like that. I mean the boy was always so polite and respectful. He was never sexy. I mean like *sexy*. I didn't know he had it in him. But damn, I swear I need to throw some ice down my shirt. I've always thought he was beautiful, but he couldn't compete with Beau in sex appeal because he was so . . . good. But wow oh wow, was he dripping with it just now. I'd have jumped in his arms if he'd done that to me, and *I* have a boyfriend."

I dropped my hands and let Leann's words sink in.

"Think about it. Did you ever see him touch or look at Ashton in a way that insinuated he wanted to get her alone? Nope, you didn't. Because it never happened. He acted like she was a nun and he was the priest. But with you just now"— Leann waved her hand toward me and grinned wickedly— "he was *hot*."

"Really?" I asked incredulously.

"Yes, really! Question is: What're you doing with Ethan? Because he's a good guy. I don't want to see him hurt, and he seems to really like you."

Shaking my head, I walked over to the sink. "I don't know, I mean I don't like him that way or anything. He's just a nice guy, and he seems interested in me, and I thought . . ." I trailed off. Ethan was her friend, and I wasn't sure being honest about why I'd said okay to a date with Ethan was a good idea.

"You thought Sawyer would get jealous. I already figured that out. We're females, Lana. It happens when a god like Sawyer Vincent unleashes his power on us. Just let Ethan down easy. Don't hurt him, okay?"

I nodded and lifted my gaze to stare at my reflection in the mirror. Who was that girl looking back at me? Did I even know her anymore? Not only did she look different, she was acting completely different.

"I won't hurt him. I'll make sure he understands, and I won't ignore him for Sawyer tonight either."

Leann nodded. "Good."

The door opened behind me, and Ashton walked in, worrying her bottom lip between her teeth as she looked from Leann to me.

"I had to run some interference, but I think everything is smoothed out now," Leann informed Ashton as she walked tentatively into the restroom.

"Oh, okay." She studied me a moment. "Are you all right?"

"Yes. I'm good."

"Sawyer is different with her Ash," Leann said bluntly.

"I know. I've noticed."

"I think it's more than he even realizes."

Ashton looked at Leann and a small smile touched her lips. "You think?"

Leann nodded. "Yep."

Ashton reached for my hand and squeezed it. "Come on. Let's get back out there before one of them says the wrong thing and all hell breaks loose."

Chapter 10

SAWYER

"What the hell was that?" Ethan demanded as soon as Ashton was out of hearing distance.

"Ash going to the restroom," I drawled in a bored tone.

Ethan started to stand up and snarled at me.

"Sit down," Beau barked, and Ethan lowered himself back into his chair. "You know what he means, Sawyer."

"He knows I like Lana. Hell, he was with us all day on the boat. She was with me. *Me.* She wants to be with me. You can see it all over her face. Not my fault he asked her out and she was too nice to turn him down."

Ethan let out a frustrated sigh. He knew I was right. "You're still hung up on Ash—" he cut himself off when Beau turned his angry glare his way.

"No, I'm not hung up on Ash. She's moved on, and I'm trying to do the same thing. But you're stepping in my way."

"Do you have to flirt with her on my date? Could you at least let me enjoy tonight with her?"

Shaking my head, I picked up the Coke the waitress had placed in front of me. "And let her think I don't care she's with you? No can do. She needs to know what I want."

Beau cleared his throat and stood up. "Hey, baby." He pulled the chair out beside him for Ashton to sit in as she walked toward the table.

I turned my head to watch as Lana walked up to the table, shifting her eyes from me to Ethan. I'd strategically taken the spot at the end of the table when Ethan had sat down, leaving the spot next to the end open for Lana.

"I'm guessing that seat isn't for me," Leann said in an amused tone under her breath as she passed me to go sit on the other side of Ashton.

Lana pulled her chair out and sat down, putting herself equidistant from Ethan and me. Sliding my chair over, I closed the distance between us until my thigh was resting against hers.

"Hey," I said quietly as she peeked at me through the curtain of her hair. I reached up and tucked the silky locks, which were blocking my view, behind her ear. "There. That's better."

Her posture tensed.

"You gonna eat those oysters with me?" I asked, leaning down to look at her menu instead of opening mine.

"Oh, I-I, uh," she stammered, and Leann let out a loud sigh.

"Tone that down a little bit would ya? The girl is so rattled she can't even talk."

I didn't take my eyes off Lana. "Am I making you nervous?"

Lana lifted her eyes to meet my gaze. A small, apologetic smile touched her lips. The pale pink lip gloss she was wearing made them appear even plumper than normal. I leaned in and caught a small whiff of the raspberry scent.

"A little," she replied softly.

She was on a date with Ethan, and I was making it very hard for her to be comfortable. The guilt that came with that knowledge stopped me from leaning in and taking a small nibble of those raspberry-flavored lips.

"I'm sorry. I'll stop," I said softly enough so that only she could hear me. I heard Ashton's voice in the background as she talked to the others, attempting to draw the attention away from Lana and me.

"Thank you," she replied and then turned her gaze back to the menu in front of her. Sliding my chair to a proper distance, I refused to look back at her as I ordered my food and carried on a conversation with everyone. I did my best not to let my gaze linger on her or lower my voice when I spoke directly to her. I even managed to eat a meal while I watched Beau kiss Ashton's hand, bare shoulder, and temple whenever he had the chance.

"That's the Sawyer I remember. I wondered where you'd run off to," Leann whispered as she walked beside me to the stadium seating at the Wharf. Ash and Beau led the way, and Ethan and Lana were behind us. I didn't turn around and check on them. I wasn't sure I could handle it if I caught them touching in any way.

"What do you mean?" I asked, only because I needed a distraction.

"Hot-and-bothered Sawyer is a new one. I've never seen you treat a girl like you could eat her up if given the chance. It was . . . interesting."

"You think Lana has me hot and bothered?"

Leann let out a cackle. "I *know* Lana has you hot and bothered. If the girl was to crook her finger your way, you'd have her pressed up against the first hard surface you could find."

I slowed my pace and glanced down at Leann. "What?"

"Don't act like you don't know what I'm talking about. You want that girl. Sweet, prim, and proper Lana went and got all sexy, and she's getting under your skin. You never did that with

Ash. Not once did I see you look at her like you wanted her. She was your trophy or possession, and you were real proud of her, but she didn't make your body simmer."

Clenching my jaw, I glared down at Leann. "You have no idea what you're talking about. I loved Ashton like crazy. She was my world. I planned my future around her. She was never a trophy or possession. Just because I didn't treat her like a piece of hot ass didn't mean she wasn't my reason for living. I respected her. I'd never treat her with anything less than respect. I'm not in danger of falling in love with someone like Lana. She's a distraction. Sure, I treat her differently; she is different, but she's just for fun."

The wide-eyed expression on Leann's face as she glanced to her right and left alerted me to the fact that I'd stopped walking and raised my voice. I turned my head to the right and saw Ashton and Beau both looking at me. Beau's expression was anything but pleased, and Ash looked like she was about to cry. *Well, hell.*

Lana.

Turning my head to the left, I saw Lana's big green eyes glistening with unshed tears as she stared at me. Ethan was glaring at me with a murderous expression.

"Lana." I started toward her, and she shook her head at me and ran off. I took a step to chase after her when Ethan stepped in front of me.

"No. I won't let you do this to her. I thought maybe you were sincere, and I was willing to step down and let you have her. But you're not. If you were, you'd never have been able to yell what you just did without a thought of her hearing you."

"Get out of my way, Ethan." I started to shove past him when a large hand clamped down on my shoulder.

"You need to let him go to her. You've done enough." Beau wouldn't let me go. I'd have to fight him first, and that would just get us both thrown in jail.

Sagging in defeat, I turned and stalked toward the car. Once the concert got going and Beau was distracted, I'd find her. I'd fix this. I had to.

The hurt look in her eyes was more painful than I would have ever imagined.

LANA

"Lana, wait," Ethan called out from behind me. As much as I didn't want him to see me crying over Sawyer, I couldn't exactly keep running away from him. He was my date. Slowing, I stopped and leaned back against the brick wall outside the restrooms.

Ethan stopped in front of me, and the worried expression on his face made me feel even worse.

"Lana, I'm sorry."

"For what? You didn't do anything but make the mistake of asking me out on a date."

He reached out, touched the side of my face, and wiped away tears with his finger. "Nothing about asking you out was a mistake."

I let out a sad laugh. "Yeah, right."

"I mean it." He sighed and dropped his hand to grab one of mine. "I realized today on the boat that you liked Sawyer. The rest of the female population in Grove has a thing for Sawyer, except for Ash, so that wasn't a big deal. I still wanted my chance. I didn't expect Sawyer to find a way to come too."

I'd been stupid enough to believe he had come because of me. It was sad, how deluded I'd been. "I'm an idiot," I whispered through the lump in my throat.

"No, you're smart, beautiful, and funny."

I smiled up at him and wiped the rest of the tears from my face. "Thank you."

"You gonna be okay?"

"Yes, I just need a little alone time. If that's okay."

Ethan nodded. "Sure, I'll meet you back at our seats."

"All right."

I washed my face with the cold water from the bathroom sink and dried my skin with a paper towel. My makeup was gone, and the freckles I worked so hard to cover up were standing out like a neon sign against my red face. I had makeup in my purse, but I'd left it in the car. Sawyer had more than likely locked it, but then again these southern Alabama people rarely locked their vehicles. I needed to walk and get my mind off things. I could at least check the car and give my red face time to return to its natural pale color.

I searched for row D and headed down until I saw the back of Sawyer's mother's Mercedes. Turning in between the cars, I didn't notice that the car door was open until Sawyer was right in front of me.

"Lana," he said in a surprised tone.

Backing up, I started to turn so I could run back to the bathroom and cry a little more, because he was just so perfect it hurt to look at him

"Lana, please, don't go. I need to talk to you."

"You've said enough."

"Lana." Sawyer grabbed my arm and firmly turned me around and backed me up against the car door. "I need you to listen to me," he pleaded, and cupped my face in his hands, gently rubbing my cheeks with the pads of his thumbs.

"I'm an asshole," he started, and I fought the urge to nod in agreement. "I didn't mean any of that the way it sounded. It wasn't even about you or how you make me feel."

"Really? Because it sure sounded like it," I blurted out.

"Leann was accusing me of never loving Ashton. She was saying that I thought of her as a possession or trophy. It set me off." He closed his eyes and let out a frustrated sigh. "With you, things are different. I'm not sure what it is, but when I'm with you, I feel something I've never felt before. I do want you. Badly. It surprises me and scares the shit out of me. Maybe I'm not good for you. Maybe what I feel is wrong. Because I did love Ashton. She was all I needed . . . but never did I feel the uncontrollable desire to get her underneath me." His voice dropped. "Never did I make up reasons to get her to wrap her legs around me so I could feel her pressed up against me. Never." He swallowed hard. "Never did I think about being inside her."

I forgot to breathe as I stared up at him. He looked torn between fear and longing. The sweet guy I'd fallen in love with years ago was there, but he was underneath the other guy he was slowly changing into.

"I'm not good for you. I don't know why you make me want you so badly. I was angry with myself when I said all that earlier. I was mad because I wanted you in a way I'd never experienced before. Before you, I just wanted to excel in football and school. I wanted my parents to be proud of me. But now, I want other things too. You get to me in a way I don't understand."

I stood up on my tiptoes and stopped his words with my

lips, but before he could pull me against him, I stepped back and broke it. "Thank you for explaining it to me," I replied as his eyes searched my face for an answer to why I'd kissed him and backed away so quickly. "I know you loved—or love—Ashton. I watched you grow up adoring her. It's just that . . . I'm not sure I can handle you flirting with me one moment and the next sulking or having angry outbursts over Ashton and Beau."

"Fair enough," Sawyer said as he reached down and threaded his fingers through mine. "I'm not ready for any kind of relationship, but I'd like to enjoy this summer. Before you came into town, I wasn't sure if I was even going to hang around until August. Now you're here, and I don't want to leave anymore. I'd like to enjoy this last carefree summer with you."

That wasn't exactly what I'd hoped for when I'd decided to come here, but it was a lot more than I expected. Maybe Sawyer would find a way to move on soon. Besides, we needed time to get to know each other without Ashton between us.

"I'd like that too."

SAWYER

Ashton's eyes went wide with surprise when she spotted Lana and me walking together toward them. She was standing in front of Beau with his arms wrapped protectively around her. I tore my attention from her and quit trying to read her facial expressions. That was something I needed to stop doing. Beau's head turned to see what Ashton was staring at, then he raised his eyebrows and shook his head once before turning back to watch the stage where Little Big Town was singing "Boondocks."

"I'm here with Ethan," Lana said.

"I know." But that didn't mean I liked it.

Her small hand grabbed mine and squeezed it before letting go quickly and walking toward Ethan, who finally noticed she was back. His worried frown went from her to me, and the angry glare directed my way wasn't lost on me. He didn't like she'd come back with me. I couldn't blame him. I hated seeing Lana's face all red and splotchy from crying. I'd walked with her to the bathroom after she retrieved her purse from the car. She'd gone inside and covered up a good bit of those adorable freckles.

I didn't follow her. She was Ethan's date; the only one he got with her. Because he was my friend and I really needed a little distance from Lana after the conversation we'd had by the car, I was going to spend the rest of the night talking to Leann and enjoying the music.

Leann studied me as I made my way over to stand beside her. Before she could open her mouth and ask twenty questions that were none of her business, I informed her: "Don't want to talk about it."

She closed her mouth and gave me a dirty look before focusing her attention on whatever Ethan was saying to Lana. I didn't allow myself even a glance over at them.

Chapter 11

LANA

Music played somewhere in the distance as I spun in circles searching for it. Just before I twirled off a huge cliff and plunged to my death, my eyes snapped open. I stared at the ceiling. The music was much louder now. Colbie Caillat was letting me know I had a phone call. Groaning, I reached for my phone on the pillow beside me. I'd gone to sleep hoping to get a text from Sawyer, but one never came.

Why was my mother calling at seven-thirty in the morning? "Mom?"

"Hey, honey, I'm sorry to wake you, but I wanted to call you before your stupid father did. You need to hear this from me and not him. He has absolutely not one drop of compassion for others. He just goes around hurting people and doing whatever his sorry ass wants to do. Selfish man. He hasn't called you, has he? Because if he has already called, I'm going to jump on a plane and fly to New York City and kick his—"

"Mom, could you tell me what's going on please?" I'd pulled myself up to a sitting position while my mother had rambled on about my father. That was her favorite pastime: coming up with names for my dad.

"Sorry. I got carried away." She sighed into the phone. "Your dad is getting married, Lana, to that new whore of his."

I was prepared for this, maybe not so soon, but I knew he had moved away to be near some woman he'd met on a business trip. I was hoping to visit him one week this summer if he found time in his schedule. It sounded pathetic that I was hoping he could pencil in time for me, but he was my dad. Up until last year, he'd lived in my house. I'd hated him at first, but eventually I'd wanted a relationship with him again.

"Okay . . . ," I began, trying carefully to filter my words while talking to my mother. She went crazy if I ever defended him. I didn't like her reminding me that he'd left me, too, whenever I tried to take up for him. Because she was right: He had left me, too, but he loved me. I knew he did. He'd told me the day he signed the divorce papers that he'd stayed with her until I had grown up. He had been planning to leave her the moment I went off to college, but things had happened and he'd had to leave a little earlier. He'd said that none of it was because of me.

He loved me and was proud of me. I needed to believe that. I held on to that at night when I lay in bed and heard my mother crying and screaming as she threw things across her bedroom.

"We knew he was serious when he moved out there to be with her. When is he planning on getting married?"

"I most certainly did not expect your forty-seven-year-old father to marry his twenty-three-year-old slut! What will people think? He's ruining our reputation. People in this town will find out and they *will* talk. You won't be able to walk around town without people whispering behind your back. This is going to *ruin* us, Lana. Just ruin us!"

Twenty-three? I cringed. What was my dad doing engaged to a girl only five years older than I was? That was just . . . gross. My mother continued to rant and call my dad names as I sat there staring at the wall in front of me. The message "Home Is Where the Heart Is" was stenciled on a framed painting hanging on the pale blue wall, mocking me. *Home? What is home now?* My mother's house where there was never any peace? My dad's apartment in Manhattan? It was about five hundred square feet, and he was going to move in with his college-age wife. Tears stung my eyes as the smell of coffee wafted down the hall to my room. I could hear my aunt and uncle chatting happily in the kitchen, and I could smell bacon frying on the stove. This was a home, one like I'd never really known.

"Did you hear me, Lana?"

Shaking myself out of the pity party I was having, I cleared my throat. "Sorry, Mom, what was that?"

"He wants to fly you to New York City to be in the wedding. Can you believe that? My baby in New York. I told him no way. You wouldn't want to be in his ridiculous wedding. But he insisted that he'd talk to you first. Be ready for that call today. The little floozy wants you to be the maid of honor. You haven't even met her."

"Okay, Mom. Thank you for letting me know. I need to go. I'll call you later. Ashton is waiting on me to go for a morning run." Mom bought my lie, and I fell back against the pillow as I ended the call.

Could this get any more screwed up? The house phone rang, and I heard my aunt answer it. I didn't have to pick up to know it was my mother telling my aunt everything she'd just told me. If mom mentioned the lie I'd told her about running with Ashton, I knew my aunt would cover for me. She understood. She always had. I snuggled down into the covers and closed my eyes. *For now, I can pretend this is my home, that I have a safe, happy place.*

As I walked into the kitchen several hours later, the faint smell of bacon still filled the air. Ashton stood by the counter in her pajamas, hair mussed, pouring herself a cup of coffee.

"Morning," I said, stopping beside the cabinet to get myself a coffee cup.

"Oh, it's my early-morning running buddy." The teasing tone in her voice made me smile.

"Uh, yeah, sorry about that. I needed an excuse to get off the phone."

Ashton laughed and handed me the pot of coffee. "No worries. Mom covered for you according to the note she left us." She pointed to the letter lying on the bar.

I reached over and picked it up.

Good morning girls,

I hope you enjoyed your early-morning run. I have to say that when Caroline called me this morning and mentioned that you two were out running, I was a little surprised. I could have sworn I'd passed both your doors and they were closed tightly. But do not worry; I didn't share that information with my sister. She believes you both enjoyed a nice, long run before coming inside to eat some of the bacon and eggs I fried up.

Love,

Mom

I smiled to myself and laid the letter back down.

"How does your mom manage to be so cool while mine is a crazed psycho?" I asked, taking a sip of my black coffee.

Ashton didn't even deny my mother's insane tendencies. She gave me a sad frown and shrugged. "Why'd your mom call so early this morning?"

I rolled my shoulders and set my cup back down. I didn't really want to talk about it, but I knew hashing it out with someone other than my mom would make my decision easier.

"Dad's getting married."

Ashton's eyes widened, and she leaned forward on the counter, resting on both elbows and studying me for a moment. I knew she was trying to gauge my reaction to the news.

"You were expecting this, right?" she asked hesitantly.

"Yes, I was. But not so soon, and maybe not to a girl only five years older than I am."

Her jaw dropped. "Uncle Nolan is engaged to a twenty-three-year-old?"

It sounded ludicrous when she said it aloud too. My dad was not an attractive guy. Sure, I loved him, but he was old and balding. Not to mention, he had a potbelly. "Crazy, huh?"

"Yeah, real crazy . . . Are you okay? Is he going to call you?"

I wasn't sure if I had ever been okay, even when both my parents had lived at home. They'd fought constantly. Most of my memories growing up had a scene in them where my mother was screaming at my dad.

"I'm fine. He's supposed to call today. His fiancée . . . She wants me to be her maid of honor. I've never even met her. I think I'm going to ask him if I can just be his best man—woman. I think I could rock a tux."

Ashton let out a long sigh then walked around the bar to stand beside me. She wrapped her arm around my waist and squeezed. "When you want to talk, rant, or even cry, I'm here."

My eyes welled up, and I swallowed the lump in my throat. I didn't like people thinking I was weak. I'd never been one to share my emotions; I kept things inside, dealt with them on my own. But knowing someone was there and cared—it meant a lot, more than she would ever know. I rested my head against hers, and we stared out at the backyard together in silence. There wasn't much more to say. Just having someone there next to me made things so much easier.

SAWYER

Beau: What days do you have to be in Florida for practice?
Me: Three days a week, starting in July.
Beau: Bama is the same. We've really only got June to take that camping trip.

Me: I'm ready when you are.

Beau: You talked to Lana?

Me: Not today. Just got back from working out
at the field house.

Beau: Ash is spending the morning with her.
She's got some shit going on with her parents.

I stared down at Beau's last text. Lana being upset made me anxious. I wasn't sure I liked that. I didn't have time for anything more than a summer fling.

Me: I'll call her. Thanks.

Beau: Be careful with her.

I didn't respond. This wasn't his business. During the end of my relationship with Ashton he'd been more involved than he should have been, but I'd let it slide because Ash was a part of his life too. But Lana . . . She was not his concern. Throwing the phone down on the bed, I headed to the bathroom for a shower. I'd already planned out a day where I could have Lana all to myself anyway. It had been my inspiration while running up and down the bleachers one hundred times.

"Where you headed, sweetheart?" called my mom from her office as I passed it on my way to the garage. I'd hoped to sneak by her without having to answer her questions. She'd been upset when Ashton had broken up with me; she'd been even more upset when she'd found out Beau had been my replacement. We'd spent a lot of time in counseling together to deal with my dad's dishonesty and find a way to face the truth without ripping our family apart. I still wanted Dad to reach out to Beau, but he wouldn't. There was no way Beau was going to make the first move. He had a lot of well-deserved bitterness inside him where my dad was concerned.

"I'm headed to pick up Lana—you remember Ashton's cousin from Georgia. We're going to Mobile to do some shopping for camping gear and maybe catch a movie or something."

Mom tilted her head and frowned. "Isn't Lana the daughter of that crazy sister of Sarah's?"

I didn't know much about Lana's mom other than that Ashton was not a fan. Shrugging, I shoved my hands in my pockets. "Lana isn't crazy. That's all that matters."

"Hmmph . . . well, don't get too attached. The apple doesn't fall far from the tree."

My aunt Honey's voice had rung in my ears not too long ago when she'd said the same thing about my dad and Beau. Scowling, I replied, "Yeah, I realized that when I found out Dad was unfaithful and then lied about it to those he was supposed to love."

My mother's back went ramrod straight. I hated the hurt

look I'd put in her eyes. She didn't deserve my anger. She'd been a victim too.

"Sorry, Mom—"

"I shouldn't have butted into your business. You're right. Go have fun. Enjoy yourself this summer. Everything changes this fall. There's a big sea out there with lots of fish, and now you and Ashton have moved on. It's time you start sampling the variety."

Mom had loved Ashton. I think she may have even picked out our china patterns at one point. Hearing her say that I needed to start "sampling the variety" was a major step for her. I walked across the room and bent down to place a kiss on the top of her head.

"Love you," I said before turning to leave.

"I love you, too, sweet boy," she replied.

Chapter 12

LANA

"No, Daddy," I said. "It isn't that I don't want to be there. I do. It's just that I've never been in New York City, and I've never met Shandra. I'd feel more comfortable if I could bring someone with me."

"You can bring anyone but your mother," my dad said. "I don't want to have to deal with her. I do want you to make time to spend with Shandra. She really wants to get to know you. We've got some special news for you."

"Special news?"

Dad cleared his throat, covered the receiver on his phone, and spoke in a muffled voice to someone else. What other news could he have? He'd already dropped the marriage bomb on me. Surely, they weren't moving to Alpharetta. That would be disastrous. My mother would not be able to leave the house without thinking everyone was talking about her or pitying her.

"Shandra wants me to go ahead and tell you. That way you can be prepared when you get here."

"Okay . . . ," I replied, waiting with a sick knot in my stomach.

"You're going to be a big sister," he replied. His excitement was unmistakable.

"What? How? Does Shandra have a kid?" Nothing else made sense. Why would he think I'd be excited over a stepsibling I'd never get a chance to know?

"No, Shandra doesn't have a kid . . . yet. You know how. You're eighteen years old, Lana. You know how babies are made . . . don't you? I assumed your mother explained that—"

"I *know* how babies are made, Daddy. What I don't understand is . . . Wait . . . She's pregnant?" I asked in horror. My dad had gotten someone *pregnant*? He was almost fifty! Could old men do that? *Ugh! Yuck.* He was going to be like the kid's grandfather.

Dad chuckled into the phone. "Yes, Shandra is pregnant. We'd planned on getting married this Christmas. She loves Christmas in New York, but, well, the baby will be here by Christmas, so instead of waiting, we decided to go ahead and have a summer wedding."

I was speechless. How did one respond to this kind of news? I sank down on the back-door steps of Ashton's house and rested my forehead on my knees.

My dad continued to chatter on about the wedding and baby plans. They would be moving out of Manhattan and to New Jersey so that they could afford a house. I wouldn't have a room, but I could share the baby's room when I came to visit. He told me I was welcome anytime.

"Lana?" Sawyer's voice was a welcome distraction.

Lifting my head, I stared up at Sawyer who was standing in front of me with a worried frown. I wondered how much he'd heard.

"Daddy, I need to go. My, uh, friend just got here, and we have plans. I'll call you back later when I've decided what to do."

"You are coming though—"

"I'm not sure, Daddy. I need to go now. I'll call when I know." I clicked end before he could say any more. I couldn't yet stand up to leave; I needed a moment.

"You okay?" Sawyer asked, lowering himself to sit down beside me since it was obvious I wasn't about to get up.

I started to nod and ended up shaking my head instead.

His arm wrapped around my shoulders, and he pulled me up against his side. That small offer of comfort caused my eyes to fill with tears. I buried my head into the curve of his arm and tried to muffle the sobs I couldn't control.

Sawyer didn't try to offer me any encouragement or pointless words. Instead he held me tighter and dropped small kisses on my hair, temple, and forehead as I cried in his arms. I'd never really cried on anyone before. Opening myself up to sharing my emotions was new for me. The part of me that was shocked by my father's behavior was pushed aside as I soaked in all the comfort I could get. It would be fleeting, but while I had it, I would take it.

After several minutes, I managed to control my tears. Reaching up, I wiped my face. Thankfully, Dad had called me before I had a chance to put on makeup. I'd have been humiliated if I'd smeared mascara all over Sawyer's white polo shirt.

"You want to talk about it?"

Sharing with Sawyer how my dad had a pregnant twenty-three-year-old fiancée wasn't something I'd ever do. It was too much for me to take in. I didn't want to see pity in his eyes when he looked at me. I preferred the lust or attraction. If he pitied me, I wouldn't be able to deal with it.

"No," I replied, sitting back up and checking to see how wet I'd gotten his shirt.

"I'll dry," he said with a smile. I could still see the concern in his eyes as he searched my face. Part of me wanted him to know everything about me, except that a bigger part knew he'd never look at me the same if he was aware how pathetic my life really was.

"Thank you."

Sawyer leaned forward and placed a soft kiss on each corner of my mouth before covering my mouth with his. He didn't try to get me to open up for him. Instead he kept it gentle and sweet. "Mmm—I've been thinking about those sweet lips all morning," he whispered against my mouth.

Melting into him was easy and unavoidable. I couldn't seem to get enough of Sawyer. He pulled back way before I wanted him to, and he ran his hand through my hair before wrapping several curls around his fingers. "Why don't you go finish getting ready? I'm anxious to get you all to myself for the day."

My legs suddenly were in complete working order again. I stood up and smiled down at him. "Give me ten minutes."

Sawyer stood up and started to follow me inside when he stopped. "Um, yeah, uh, I think I'll just wait in the truck if that's okay."

Ashton wasn't inside. She'd left with Beau an hour ago, but I knew that wasn't why he didn't want to come inside. There had to be a lot of memories in this house that he wasn't ready to revisit right now.

"Okay, I won't be long," I assured him.

SAWYER

Pulling onto the dirt road that led out to the field seemed like a bad decision. I'd just spent the day with Lana, all alone. We'd bought her a sleeping bag, backpack, and a few other supplies for our camping trip. Then, instead of a movie, she'd talked me into playing eighteen holes of putt-putt golf. It had sounded like a stupid idea, but listening to Lana's laughter and seeing her strut around when she'd gotten a hole-in-one had been more entertaining than any movie.

"I haven't been to one of these since . . ." She trailed off, biting her bottom lip.

At the last field party Lana had gone to, she'd covered for Beau and Ashton. When I realized that Lana had known Beau and Ash were messing around behind my back and hadn't told me, I'd been upset. I'd always thought she was on my team. It wasn't her fault; I had moved on enough now to see that clearly. Reaching across the seat, I grabbed her hand.

"The last time was when Beau and Ash were messing around behind my back. Although you covered for them that night, it wasn't your fault. No worries, okay?"

She let her bottom lip pop free of her teeth; it appeared red and swollen. Well, damn, that was just too tempting. I let go of her hand, slid my hand between her thighs, and pulled her over to me.

"That's better. You were too far away," I whispered before I bent my head so that I could pull her bottom lip into my mouth and gently suck on it. The surprised little noise she made had me pulling her closer. I let my hand slip farther between her bare legs and squeeze the soft skin of her thigh in my hand.

Lana pressed her chest against mine and made a pleading

noise in her throat. Picking her leg up, I draped it over my knee and slid my hand up a little higher inside her thigh. Her breathing hitched, and I realized my heart was racing the closer I got to the edge of her underwear.

"No, don't," Lana said breathlessly as she gave me a gentle push breaking the kiss. She quickly slid her leg off my knee and closed her legs. I'd been really close to doing something I hadn't done but once in my life, when I'd been in seventh grade and had been a little confused as to why Nicole wanted me to touch her underwear.

"I'm sorry," I said, sitting back in my seat and focusing on the trees in front of me instead of checking to see if she was mad at me—or worse, terrified. I needed to get ahold of my pounding heart first. I'd been so close, and she'd been so warm.

"Don't be sorry. I just . . . I've never done anything like that before, and I got a little nervous. I'm not sure I'm ready for that."

Her small hand covered mine, and my tightened fist released under her touch.

"Me either," I replied, finally turning to meet her eyes.

Her eyes widened in surprise. "You either—what?"

I let out a chuckle and flipped my hand over so that our palms were touching. Then I threaded my fingers through hers. "I've never done anything like that before. Unless you count in seventh grade when Nicole locked us in Kayla's closet during a game of spin the bottle and forced me to touch her panties or she'd tell the whole school I was too scared to kiss her."

A small bubble of laughter escaped Lana's mouth, and she slapped her free hand over it to keep from laughing out loud. I smiled and squeezed her hand. It was a funny story.

"Let me tell you. What we almost did blew that very strange and disturbing memory out of the water."

This time the laughter was too loud to cover up with her hand, and I reached over and pulled it from her mouth. "Don't. I like to hear you laugh. And that is one helluva funny story. So laughing is expected."

"I can't believe Nicole threatened you," she said, still laughing softly.

"Really? Have you met Nicole? She was determined to lose her virginity before high school if at all possible. I think Beau may have helped her reach that goal in eighth grade."

"Oh, my." Her laughter faded away and a serious thoughtful expression replaced it.

"What's going through that head of yours now?"

A forced smile immediately appeared on her lips. "Nothing, sorry." She glanced out at the bonfire in the distance between the pecan trees. "You ready to get out?"

She was very closed off about a lot of things. The more she didn't want to tell me, the more I wanted to know about her.

Her phone began singing some sappy love song I'd heard before on the radio, and she reached into her purse and pulled it out. Instead of answering it, she quickly turned it off and slipped it back inside the pocket of her purse.

"No one important?" I asked, wanting her to share some-thing, anything, with me.

She shook her head and reached for the door handle. "Nope. No one I can't call back later."

I watched as she jumped down out of my truck before I got out on my side. Lana McDaniel held everything close. I wondered if I'd ever really know what she was thinking.

Sitting on the tailgate of Jake's truck with Lana tucked between my legs, I was satisfied. Ash curled up in Beau's lap wasn't even on my radar. I'd managed to talk to everyone, Beau included. We discussed football, college, and our camping trip without any problems. It was nice. Lana was nice. No, Lana was more than nice. Having her in my arms made everything bearable.

"Heads up. Kyle and Nic just got here," Ethan said, before taking another swig of his beer. Nicole hadn't been around much since Beau and Ash had hooked up. She'd made a go for me a few times. Once, I'd even been tempted to take her out to my truck one night and just screw her. Get it over with. But I couldn't do it. I didn't want my first time to be with Nicole in the back of my truck at a field party. I'd waited this long—I could wait longer. Ash was supposed to have been my one and only. But that plan was over. I figured one day the right girl would come along, and when that happened, the place wouldn't be important—just as long as it was with the one person I couldn't live without.

"She's coming this way," Kayla said smugly. The girl loved drama. With Nicole around, drama was bound to follow.

"You wanna go, baby?" Beau asked Ashton, starting to shift so she could up.

"No. I'm not scared of Nicole, Beau. What's she going to do to me? Hmm?" Beau chuckled and leaned in to give Ashton a kiss on the nose. My chest ached only slightly at the sight of them, but nothing like the times in the past when I'd been unable to take a deep breath when he kissed her.

"Well, look at the Vincent boys. Getting along. Both of you all snuggled up to girls, no one trying to beat up the other one. Looks like Sawyer has moved on, Ash," Nicole drawled out as she winked at me and sauntered over to stop in front of Lana who stood in her way.

"Since you've gotten over your Ashton depression, why don't you and I go out one night and have some fun?"

Lana tensed in my arms. A protective streak coursed through me, and I pulled her up against me tightly, placing my hands on her hips. "I'll have to pass, Nic. I've already found someone to spend time with this summer."

Nicole smirked as she let her gaze travel up and down Lana as if she wasn't impressed. "You can do much better."

"I disagree."

"You need someone with experience after wasting all

those years with the preacher's daughter."

I heard Ashton ordering Beau to calm down and ignore Nicole.

"I'm not into overused merchandise. I've got standards, you know."

The surprised laugh from Lana had me smiling like an idiot. I loved making her laugh. She'd relaxed and leaned into me when I'd tightened my hold on her. Knowing I made her feel safe and unthreatened was a heady feeling.

"Once the Vincent boys were the hottest thing around. You've not lived up to your potential. You're both boring. One day you'll crave that excitement you missed out on," Nicole said with a snarl before flipping her dark brown hair over her shoulder and walking over to Kyle, who had stood silently while watching her make a play for me.

"Come on, Kyle, I've had enough of this place." She stalked past him, and Kyle threw me an apologetic look before following her.

"Why does he put up with that?" Ashton asked as they walked away.

"Because she's an easy lay," Jake replied.

Chapter 13

LANA

"If you're going to sleep in Beau's tent, then who is going to sleep with me?" I asked. "I don't want to sleep in a tent all by myself. There are black *bears* in the Cheaha Mountains. I know this for a fact because I googled it."

Ashton threw me a saucy smile over her shoulder. "Well, I'm sure you could share a tent with Sawyer. I have no doubt he'd rather share with you than Jake."

I flopped down on her bed and groaned in frustration. Sharing a tent with Sawyer would be difficult. We'd been on two dates since the field party, and not once had we done anything more than kiss. After I'd put the brakes on his hand slowly creeping up my thigh, he'd been hands-off on my body.

"He hasn't offered that, and I am not asking him. Can I get a lock for my tent?"

Ashton laughed and threw another pair of shorts on her bed to pack. "Bears can't unzip tents, Lana."

"Well, chainsaw psychos who wander the woods looking for young girls all alone to chop up into pieces can," I replied.

"There are no chainsaw psychos! I can't believe you've never been camping. It's safe, Lana. I promise."

"Easy for you to say. You'll be snuggled up safely in the arms of Beau Vincent. I'm more than positive he could take on a black bear," I muttered.

Ashton pulled a large, red backpack out of her closet that was very similar to the royal blue one that Sawyer had helped me pick out. The excitement for our upcoming trip made me wish I could share in her joy. But every time I tried to get excited, visions of black bears, snakes, and chainsaws haunted my thoughts.

"Stop frowning. You'll be fine. I'll get someone to share a tent with you. You won't be left alone."

Reaching for the tiny little bikini Ashton had dropped on the bed, I picked it up and raised an eyebrow in surprise. "So, I'm guessing your mom hasn't seen this one?"

Ashton rolled her eyes and snatched it out of my hand before glancing back at the door to make sure it was still closed. "No, she hasn't. I bought it for this trip."

"I just bet you did," I teased.

Ashton frowned. "Shh ... Do you not remember all the begging I had to do to make this happen? The only saving graces we have are the facts that *Sawyer* is going to be there and they believe you and I are sharing a tent. And I might have left out the fact Beau will be there."

"Ashton! You did not! What if they talk to his mother?" I asked, horrified.

"That ain't gonna happen. My parents and Honey Vincent aren't exactly chummy."

"Okay, if you say so," I replied just as my phone alerted me that I had a new text message.

Sawyer: What're you doing?

Me: Watching Ash pack.

Sawyer: Why aren't you packing?

Me: B/c I'm stressing over the black bears that are going to eat me in my sleep.

Sawyer: HA! No black bears will eat you. They don't do redheads. You're safe.

Me: Very funny. I happen to know that they aren't very picky and that there are plenty of them in Cheaha.

Sawyer: Naw, I've never seen one there.

Me: Well, they're there. Google it.

Sawyer: I'll keep you safe.

Me: Maybe during the day, but at night, when I'm alone in my tent, they'll come for me.

Sawyer: Alone in your tent? Um, no. You're in my tent.

I lifted my head to see Ashton watching me as I texted back and forth with Sawyer.

She was amused to say the least. "Well, what's he saying?"

"That I'm sharing his tent."

Ashton raised her eyebrows. "Told ya."

Me: Are you sure?

Sawyer: Hell yeah, I'm sure. Why do you think I'm going on this camping trip?

Me: Um . . . because you like to sleep on hard, rocky ground and get chased by bears?

Sawyer: Funny. Go take your cute little ass to your room and get packing.

Me: Yes, sir.

"Oh, ye of little faith," Ashton said in a singsong voice as I stood up and slipped my phone into the pocket of my shorts.

"Yeah, yeah, you know everything," I replied.

"You going to go pack now?"

"Yes, I guess I need to get on that. Do we really have to leave so early in the morning, though?"

"Afraid so. It's a five hour drive then we need to hike up to our camping spot and put up our tents before the sun goes down."

It was still dark outside when Sawyer drove up in the Suburban that belonged to his dad. It had room for eight. That way we could all drive up together.

I'd packed as much clothing as I could fit in my backpack. Ashton had assured me there were showers on the grounds we could use. I was not about to get in snake-infested water to wash up.

"Good morning, sunshine," Sawyer said as I stumbled out the door. We had overslept, and there had been no time to make coffee.

My eyes focused on the Styrofoam cup in his hand as he extended it to me. "You drink it black, right?"

"Come here," I said, grabbing a handful of the black T-shirt he was wearing until he was close enough for me to kiss. I laid a very loud smack on his mouth before taking the cup from his hands. "You're my hero."

"If I'm going to get that kind of greeting, I may just start showing up every morning with a cup of coffee in hand,"

Sawyer drawled in a sexy voice as he slipped his hand around my waist.

"We need to load up. Back away from the girl, lover boy, and help out," Jake grumbled as he took my backpack and sleeping bag from the front porch and headed to the Suburban.

Sawyer chuckled and picked up the extra duffel bag that Ash and I had packed with a few things we couldn't fit in our backpacks. He looked at me and raised his eyebrows in question.

"The backpacks didn't have enough room in them. Besides, that isn't all mine. Ashton and I both needed a few more things," I explained.

"You're breaking a camping rule, but because you look so amazingly hot in those little hiking shorts, I'll overlook it."

I put the steaming cup of coffee to my lips to hide the silly grin on my face. Who would have known Sawyer Vincent could be so good at flirting?

"What's with the duffel?" Toby demanded as Sawyer threw it up to him so he could strap it on top of the vehicle.

"Ash and Lana had a few things that wouldn't fit in their backpacks. Shut up and strap it down," Sawyer replied, and turned back to look at me with a cocky grin.

"Kayla tried this, and I made her take it back inside," Toby complained.

"Ain't our fault you're a sucky boyfriend, Toby. Now strap the duffel down," Beau said in an annoyed tone as he walked around from the backside of the Suburban.

I made my way over to the SUV to get in but stopped because I wasn't sure if I should assume I was riding in the front with Sawyer. I searched the yard for Ashton, but it was still dark out and the front porch light only lit up part of the yard.

"So, you're Sawyer's new girl?" an unfamiliar voice asked from behind me. I spun around to see a petite girl with a headful of pale blond hair that stuck out in wild ringlets everywhere. Her eyes were a bright blue, so startling that she had to be wearing contacts. She had a golden tan that didn't at all match up with the pale color of her hair. But she was really pretty.

"Um, yes. Well, no. We're just friends," I replied.

She rolled her eyes. "You aren't just friends. Sawyer doesn't kiss his friends. If he did, I'd be lined up waiting for my turn. I've been his friend since kindergarten and not once has he kissed me."

"Oh" was the only response I had for her. It was too early, and I hadn't finished my coffee yet. My verbal skills were lacking.

"I'm Heidi. Kayla is one of my best friends. We cheered together all four years of high school. Jake and I have an on-again-off-again thing going. Right now it's on." She winked at me and took a sip from her Thermos.

"You getting in? I think Jake and I are going to take the back"—she paused and looked around—"unless Beau and Ash are taking it. Don't think I'm up for the Beau Vincent love marathon the whole way."

"Are four people sitting in the back? Won't that be crowded?"

Heidi frowned as if that had just dawned on her. "Oh, I guess we can't all sit in pairs."

I still really wasn't sure where I should sit. Sawyer came up beside me and opened the passenger side door. "You're sitting up here with me. If I have to drive the whole way, I at least deserve to have you to entertain me."

That answered my question.

Heidi tilted her head back to look at Toby and Jake strapping luggage down on top of the Suburban. "So how are we sitting? I'm ready to get in, and I don't know where to go."

"Ash and I are in the back. Someone will have to ride back there with us if we're all going to fit," Beau informed her as he opened the door and helped Ash inside.

"Jake, you're in the back beside Beau. Heidi can sit with Kayla and me in the middle," Toby piped up.

"Why do I have to get stuck in the back by Beau? Why can't you?" Jake snapped.

"Because Kayla is my girlfriend. Heidi is your fuck-buddy," Toby replied, jumping down and checking the straps one more time with a hard tug.

"Hey! Don't call me that!" Heidi yelled.

Toby shrugged. "Sorry, Heidi, I call 'em like I see 'em. If the two of you ever make it exclusive, I'll be sure to change my opinion."

"What I can't believe is you just said *fuck* in the pastor's yard." Jake smirked as he walked around the corner of the vehicle toward us.

Sawyer leaned down and whispered in my ear. "They're going to argue about this for a few more minutes. Go ahead and get in."

He held my hand and helped me up. I loved how he made me feel special when he did little things like that. "I'll stop by a Starbucks and get you some more coffee as soon as we get out of Grove," he promised before closing the door.

SAWYER

Lana was holding her fresh cup of coffee close to her nose, smelling it at her leisure. I'd decided to drive through Mobile just so we could find a Starbucks. She was much more awake and alert than when she'd staggered out of the house earlier in a sleepy haze. I'd wanted to cuddle her up and take her back to bed, but that wasn't something I could act on. She'd drawn a line with us physically, and I was trying to stay behind that line. But the more time we spent together made it harder and harder.

"Why is it that Starbucks coffee just smells better than anything you can make at home?" she asked, cutting her eyes over in my direction with a flirty bat of her lashes. If it weren't for the fact that I already knew the girl had no clue how to flirt, I'd think it was on purpose. The more I got to know her, the more I realized that she really had no idea how tempting she was.

"It's a head game. They do an excellent job of marketing," I replied, reaching for my cup and taking a long swig before setting it back in the cupholder.

"Hmm . . . I don't know. I've tried buying the Starbucks brand at the grocery store and making it at home, but it doesn't smell the same."

I started to reply, but Jake yelled out. "There's not enough room in this backseat for me and Beau! We're cramped up. Heidi and I need to switch spots."

"Just stick Ash in your lap, Beau, and scoot over," I replied, glancing over at Lana, who was staring at me with a surprised look in her eyes. Winking, I reached for her hand.

"What is it?" I asked.

She just shook her head and smiled at me.

"Ah! God, that is so much better," Jake said, groaning loudly.

"Throw me my pillow, Heidi. I'm going to need to go to sleep. Ash in Beau's lap is going to get out of hand soon enough, and I'd rather not watch."

My stomach tightened at his words but only for a second. It hadn't bothered me to suggest Ash sit in Beau's lap, but the idea of him touching her still got to me. Threading my fingers through Lana's, I focused on the road and the fact Lana would be cuddled up to me in my tent for the next three nights.

The tents were all set up, and the fire was blazing brightly by the time the sun set over the Cheaha Mountains. The girls had all hiked to the bathrooms to take showers. We'd had to move camp closer to the public bathhouse than I preferred, but Ashton had pouted when I suggested we move out another mile. Beau had dropped everything in his hands, and without looking to me or anyone else for agreement, he began setting up camp. Ash had never pouted to me when she wanted her way. It was strange to see her voice an opinion. It was even weirder to watch Beau give in to someone so easily. She really was different with him. She didn't bend to his will and ask him what he wanted first. The free-spirited little girl who would rather throw water balloons at cars, roll yards with toilet paper, and sneak out of her bedroom window to go comfort the trashy barmaid's son was back. She'd just needed

Beau to help her find herself again. A lump formed in my throat at the realization that it was my fault she'd lost herself. I walked out of the firelight and into the darkness to stare out at the shadowed nature around us. Pressing a hand against my chest, I rubbed hard, forcing the emotion tightening my chest to go away.

Just when I thought things were getting better with how I felt about Ashton, something always happened to send me spiraling back into the pain. Granted, it was getting easier, and it wasn't anything near what it was in the beginning—but it wasn't completely gone. I feared it never would be. Ashton would always be my biggest mistake. Not because I loved her but because I had lost her.

"You good?" Beau's voice broke into the silence around me. Dropping my hand from my chest, I stuck it into my pocket and nodded without turning to look back at him.

"What're you doing out here? Getting away from Jake's bitching?"

"Just looking around," I replied.

Beau stopped beside me. From my peripheral vision, I could see him staring out in the same direction as me.

"You seem happy with Lana. Ash said Lana really likes you."

I could hear the silent warning in his voice. If I hurt Lana, I hurt Ashton, and Beau wouldn't be okay with that.

"Lana is great. She knows where I stand. August will be

here soon, and I'll be going to Florida and she'll be going . . . wherever it is she's going."

Beau turned his head to look at me. "You don't even know where she's going to college?"

"No. It's never come up."

Beau shook his head. "Once, not too long ago, you were the good brother. You were careful with everyone's feelings. It was fucking ridiculous how polite and thoughtful you were. You've changed, man. Can't believe I'm saying this, but I miss that guy. He was someone I always admired. I couldn't be proud of my choices, but I was always so damn proud of yours."

The anger that had surfaced instantly was gone with that last sentence. Beau turned and walked back to the campsite, leaving me there to think about what he'd said. Knowing he'd been proud of me made my eyes burn. That wasn't something I ever imagined my tough-ass brother admitting.

Chapter 14

LANA

I sat on my sleeping bag, checking my text messages that had magically appeared when we'd made it to the bathhouse. Reception out there in the wilderness wasn't so good. But there was wi-fi at the bathhouse, which was both surprising and kind of funny. Sawyer, Beau, and Toby were still putting out the fire and making sure all our supplies were packed up safely for the night. We'd sat around the fire and roasted weenies and marshmallows. Sawyer had packed a few cold things in a cooler that we had to use that night because by the next night the ice would have melted and everything would've been ruined. I didn't even want to think about what we'd have to eat tomorrow night.

Dad: I need you to call me.

Dad: Please, call me, honey. I can't seem to get through to your phone.

Dad: I called the house. Sarah told me you were camping. Be safe and call me as soon as possible.

I wasn't ready to talk to him just yet. I'd have to call him once I got back to Ashton's. But right then I needed more time.

Mom: You do not have to go to New York City.

Mom: Why didn't you tell me the slut was pregnant?

Mom: I do NOT want you going up there. Your father is completely screwing up your life. Just ignore him. He can rot in hell for all I care.

Mom: Don't you call him! Sarah said he called asking where you were. And you didn't tell me you were dating SAWYER VINCENT! I'm so excited for you.

I'd finally managed to have something that had been Ashton's. My mother adored Ashton, and most of my life I'd had to hear how perfect Ashton was and how I should try to be more like her. It's no wonder I was so mean to her when we were kids. Shaking my head, I deleted the rest of her texts without reading them.

Jewel: You decide on what to do about college yet and have you even spoken to your dad about the money?

Jewel: You can ignore me, but when you're stuck in Alpharetta, commuting to the junior college while everyone else is off living a real college experience . . . you'll wish you'd done something!

She was right. I needed to talk to Dad about the money I needed. I'd gotten a small scholarship, but if I was going to go to an out-of-state college, I needed help financially. I'd been accepted and my registration was paid. The trouble was that, due to my dad's income, I couldn't get any extra money. I hadn't applied for loans in time, and I needed help.

The tent flap opened, and Sawyer ducked inside, grinning. "Waiting up for me?"

My heart fluttered, and all worries of school were pushed aside. "Yes."

"I had to slay all those hungry black bears circling the tent first," he teased.

I started to reply when he yanked his shirt over his head and his very well-defined bare chest was inches from my face. Swallowing hard, I focused on breathing properly. His abs were so perfect that they looked unreal. I mean, I'd seen him shirtless before but never this close up. His cargo shorts hung on his hips. Even his hips were defined. The small patch of dark hair that trailed from below his belly button to beneath the waist of his shorts made me gulp. Suddenly it was very, very hot in the tent, and I needed someone to throw cold water on me or fan me.

"Lana." Sawyer's voice broke into my thoughts, and I lifted my eyes from his tantalizing flat stomach to his meet his gaze. *Oh my.* Licking my lips nervously, I tried to think of a response, but Sawyer was laying me back and covering my mouth and body within seconds. His lips were gentler than the look in his eyes had been. I gasped as his bare chest brushed the thin material of my tank top and his tongue was in my mouth, teasing, tasting, and driving me crazy.

I needed to feel him. Sliding my hands up his arms, I felt him flex. Loving the powerful feeling that came with the knowledge I could affect him with just a touch, I continued my exploration of his muscular back. I grazed his mouthwatering abs with my nails, eliciting a groan from him. His mouth left mine, and he began kissing a trail from my jawline down to my neck. The closer he got to my chest, the heavier my breathing became. Holding himself over me with one arm, he took his other hand and traced the neckline of my tank top with his finger as he watched me closely. I knew he was waiting on permission to go farther, and although I knew letting him go any farther wasn't a very good idea, I couldn't tell him no. The needy gleam in his eyes was impossible to deny. For fear my voice wouldn't work, I leaned up and into his touch in response. His eyes widened in surprise, then a glazed look came over them as he lowered his head. He kept his eyes on mine until his mouth pressed onto the top of my cleavage, which was showing just above the neckline.

His green eyes held my attention as his tongue darted out and took a small lap at the swell of my breast then trailed along the top until it met the crease between the two of them. One big hand slid underneath the bottom of my top and left a sizzling hot trail up my stomach until it stopped at the underside of my bra. Something close to a whimper escaped me, and that was all the encouragement Sawyer needed. His hand slid over the lace of my bra, where he found the front clasp and quickly unsnapped it. I closed my eyes tightly as I felt both my breasts spring free. No one had ever touched me like this.

When his calloused hand covered my right breast, I almost shot straight up. The jolt that went directly to the small ache between my legs shocked me. He eased my tank top slowly up my body. If I were going to stop him, then that moment would have been the time. I opened my eyes and started to say something, but his dilated pupils and awed expression stopped me. Instead I leaned up and lifted my arms as he took the tank top and bra off me. This was it: my first time topless in front of a boy. And it wasn't just any boy; it was the only one I'd ever imagined doing this with. Every fantasy I'd ever conjured up about

Sawyer Vincent touching me held nothing to the reality of it.

"Lana," he whispered, staring down at me. I shifted, opening my legs so that he rested between them and his arousal pressed directly on the ache between my legs.

"Oh my god," I said, moaning loudly, and Sawyer's mouth was on mine. His slow, sweet kisses were gone and he consumed me with a wild urgency. My body bucked against his as if it had a mind of its own, and this time, Sawyer groaned. Both of his hands covered my bare breasts. He rolled each nipple between his thumb and forefinger, sending my world spiraling out of control. His mouth smothered my response to him, but at the moment I didn't care. It was as if someone had shot fireworks off in my body. I clung to him, afraid I might be falling somewhere I couldn't come back from. The pain had ricocheted into a pleasure I didn't know existed.

As I slowly came back to Earth, I realized two things. Sawyer was no longer touching my chest. His hands were on either side of my head, handfuls of the sleeping bag underneath me tightly in his fist. His head was buried in the curve of my neck and shoulder, and he was breathing deep and hard. His body was held rigid over mine, and I carefully unwrapped my legs from around him where I'd been holding him in a viselike lock. Sawyer didn't move or relax. Worry and embarrassment at my reaction to what we'd been doing started settling in. Was he okay? Had I just had an orgasm?

His warm mouth pressed a kiss to my neck, and I shivered underneath him. "Don't," he demanded in a hard whisper. I stilled, instantly worried I'd done something else wrong.

We lay there for a few more minutes in silence, and my concern began to grow.

Finally he slowly lifted his head to let go of his death grip on the sleeping bag and push himself up off me, careful not to put any pressure between my legs. Humiliation washed over me when I saw him reach for my tank top. Without saying anything, I let him put it on me. He pulled it down over my bare chest and stomach then quickly let go of it and sat back on his sleeping bag. I'd done something wrong. My stomach felt sick.

"I'm sorry," I whispered.

Sawyer lifted his head so he was looking in my direction, but I didn't meet his gaze. I couldn't.

"What?" he asked in a deep, husky voice I'd never heard him use.

Covering my face with my hands so he couldn't see the tears welling up in my eyes, I replied, "I don't know why I did that. I'm so sorry. I didn't mean—"

Sawyer was in front of me, pulling my hands away from my face and forcing me to look at him. "You're sorry? Lana, do you understand anything that just happened?"

I shrugged, then shook my head.

Sawyer let out a small laugh and reached to pull me onto

his lap. "That was the single most incredible moment of my life. Don't be sorry for it. Please," he said in the same low, sexy tone he'd used before.

I studied him a moment. "But . . . I don't understand."

Sawyer leaned in and kissed the tip of my nose, then each of my eyelids. "Let me explain it to you then. I just had a beautiful girl trust me enough to touch her and see her in a way no one else ever has. I got to hold her and watch her and feel her as she came apart in my arms. It was like nothing else I'd ever experienced. She was breathtaking and she was responding to me. She wanted me. I was the one making her spiral out of control."

Oh. But . . . "But you acted tense and angry when I reacted that way and moved away from me like you didn't want to be near me anymore."

Sawyer chuckled. "Lana, I was using every amount of self-control I could find to keep from pulling off those shorts of yours and going somewhere neither of us are ready to go. For a moment there, all I saw was red-hot need and I came real close to taking it. What you thought was anger was me forcing myself to calm the fuck down."

The hardness I could still feel under my butt as I sat in his lap told me he hadn't exactly calmed all the way down.

"But you're still . . ." I trailed off, and a crooked grin appeared on his face.

"Yeah, well, I doubt I'll get rid of that without a really cold shower, which I think I may need to go take in a minute."

Oh, wow. I knew enough to know a guy could go through a lot of pain if a girl worked him up enough and he didn't . . . get his release. The ache had gotten so intense before I'd broken into a million pieces. I couldn't imagine being forced to stay in that state with no end. He'd held me while I found my release.

"I could . . . help," I offered quietly, and Sawyer's body went rigid at my words.

"*What?*"

"I could help with your, um . . . need for release. I mean, it is my fault you're like this. I could . . . I mean, I want to help."

"Ah, shit," he muttered, covering his face with his hand and rubbing it hard. "Lana, you can't say things like that to me right now."

"Why?"

"Because it only makes me hurt worse thinking about it."

Crawling off his lap, I didn't raise my eyes to see what his reaction was. Instead I took a deep breath and reached for the button of his shorts. His hand grabbed mine. "Oh, no. I'm not letting you do that."

"I want to."

Sawyer shook his head. "No, Lana. I'll go up to the bathhouse and fix this."

Shoving his hand away with more strength than was required, I continued to undo his shorts.

"Oh god," he said with a groan as I pulled them down. He lifted his hips so I could pull them far enough down his hips. I was on a major power trip. Seeing Sawyer Vincent completely fascinated with everything I was doing was sexy, not to mention fun.

I pushed the nervous, reserved Lana, who was screaming in my head that I could not touch a boy *there*, far away. I reached into his boxers, and my hands felt his warm, silky erection.

"Holy shit." Sawyer exhaled so deeply that he sent shivers through me.

SAWYER

I opened my eyes as the warmth of the early morning rays hit the tent. Last night's events slowly washed over me, and the body I had pressed up against me made me smile. Lana McDaniel had rocked my world last night. When she'd come in my arms, I was pretty damn sure nothing could ever be that hot. But then the expression of awe on her face, her mouth slightly open in wonder as she gently used her innocent ministrations to give me my release, had been the absolute sexiest thing I'd ever seen.

Pulling her tighter against my chest, I inhaled the sweet, subtle scent of her shampoo, and closed my eyes.

"Good morning," she said groggily as she rolled over in my arms until she was facing me. The shy smile on her face said she knew that she'd made me a very happy man last night.

"Mornin'," I murmured before softly kissing her mouth.

She backed away and covered her mouth to keep me from doing anything more.

"Morning breath. I need to brush my teeth," she explained as she kept her hand over her mouth.

"I'm sure it smells as sweet as the rest of you," I assured her, ducking my head and kissing her neck before sniffing her skin loud enough to make her giggle. I wasn't one for giggling, but that giggle was sexy and rare. I liked it—a lot.

"Get up; we got a waterfall to find. It's gonna be hot as hell in a few hours, and we'll need to be close to the cold water to cool off when it hits." Jake's voice boomed over the campsite.

Lana pushed away from me and sat up. I rolled over on my back and watched her as she gathered her supplies to get ready.

She flashed a smile back at me as she reached for the zipper of the tent. I noticed her discarded bra from last night; I sat up and grabbed her arm.

"You can't go out there like that," I said in a more demanding voice than I'd intended. The idea of Jake or anyone else seeing her braless in that skimpy little top sent a possessive jolt through me. No way in hell.

"Like what?" She frowned, staring down at my hand on her arm.

I picked up her bra and dangled it in front of her. "You need to put this on."

She held up the clothes in her arms. "I'm putting on my swimsuit under my clothes. I don't need my bra today."

"Uh, yeah, you do. You're not walking out of this tent with your tits covered up by only that thin piece of cotton."

A smile tugged on her lips and she snatched the bra out of my hands.

Chapter 15

SAWYER

The waterfall was only a five-mile hike, which was a good thing because if I had to hear Heidi complain for one more minute, I was going to lose it.

I searched for Lana and found her sitting out on a rock across the water beside Ashton. I stood there and watched them. Ashton's laughter always made me smile. Hearing it ring out over the water as she talked happily with Lana made things feel right. Ashton had held my heart for so long that, even after her betrayal, I'd have taken her back without question if she'd asked. As much as I loved my brother, I wasn't sure I wouldn't still. My eyes shifted to Lana, who was talking now. Her happy expression made me feel like a king. She'd been in an excellent mood all morning; knowing it was because of me was nice. The memory of Lana's touch last night far exceeded anything I'd ever experienced with Ashton. I wasn't sure how I felt about that.

Ashton had owned me. I'd have moved Heaven and Earth to make her happy. It was different with Lana. I enjoyed her company, and being with her was exhilarating. But I knew what love felt like, and what I was feeling for Lana wasn't even close. The feelings I had were more intense but only physically. The idea of leaving her in August didn't ache the way it did when I thought of Ash being so far away.

"She's one hot piece of ass. If you get bored and want to trade tent buddies, just let me know." I jerked my head to glare at Jake as he stood smirking with his attention focused on Lana.

"What did you just say?" I demanded, towering over Jake by only a few inches. I fisted both my hands, prepared to knock him on his ass if he dared to repeat his crude comment.

"Whoa, Saw, calm down, bud. You do realize I wasn't talking about Ash, don't you?" Jake held up both his hands and backed away from me.

"I know who you were talking about, and I suggest you take your perverted eyes off her. She isn't up for grabs."

"Well, well, well, what the hell did you do, Jake? Not sure I've ever seen Sawyer so ready to pummel someone other than me before," Beau drawled in a lazy, amused tone.

"Shut up, Beau," I snapped, not looking back at him.

"I don't know. He's gone apes-hit. I just made a comment about Lana. Last time he talked about her, she was just a fucking 'distraction.' I didn't know he would go all territorial," Jake replied, glancing over my shoulder toward my brother. I could see the request for backup in his eyes, and it only pissed me off more.

"He's right, bro. Back off. You've been referring to Lana as a distraction for more than a week. If you've gone and changed your mind, then you might want to let everyone know."

I hated it when Beau had a valid point. He was the Neanderthal—not me. He wasn't supposed to make sense. Jerking my shirt over my head, I threw it on the rocky ground and dove into the water. I needed to be near Lana. That was the only thing that was going to calm down the violent storm inside me.

LANA

I wanted a shower before I crashed. I was exhausted. Today had been a blast, but between the heat, swimming, and hiking, I could hardly keep my eyes open. I plugged in my phone to charge and placed it on the small ledge over the sink in the bathhouse. Then I went to get cleaned up. Ash had said her head hurt and she wanted to lie down a few minutes before coming to take a shower. Heidi and Kayla both said they were too tired to walk up here and shower, which I thought was gross. They decided the water at the falls was enough of a shower for them.

I'd sweated on our hike back, and I knew they had too, but it wasn't my business. If they wanted to go to bed nasty, then so be it. Walking up here alone with the bears, snakes, and psycho chainsaw men had taken a great deal of bravery on my part.

I was also anxious to get back to Sawyer. The hope that we might have a night similar to the previous night had been at the forefront of my thoughts all day. Ashton had mentioned my silly smile, and I'd been vague with my reply as to why I was so giddy. Anyway, I was pretty sure she knew exactly why.

After finishing my shower, I dried off and slipped on my tank top—without a bra this time—and the pink-striped boxer shorts I'd brought to sleep in. It was dark, and I had to carry my supplies and dirty clothes back with me. I could hold those in front of my shirt. Sawyer would never notice I'd gone braless outside of the tent. His possessive reaction to my walking out of the tent without one this morning had surprised me. No one had ever been possessive of me. Maybe the healthy response would've been to stand my ground and force him to accept I was my own person. But I didn't. I wanted to be wanted.

Picking up my phone, I noticed missed calls and text messages. Sighing, I scrolled through them and saw my dad had called twice. My mother had called fifteen times, and then they'd both left several text messages. I needed to call one of them back. Mom would keep me on the phone forever, and I really wanted to get to that tent.

So I tapped my dad's name and waited as the phone rang.

"Finally. Is there no reception up there? I've called you several times."

"Hi, Daddy. Sorry, but yes, the reception is shoddy up here."

"I'm glad you finally got my messages and called. I need to talk to you about the wedding. There's been a change of plans."

"Okay—"

"Shandra's grandmother lives on the coast in South Carolina. She's wealthy, and her home is a historical landmark. She has offered it to Shandra to use for the wedding. Since Shandra can't have her Christmas wedding in New York, she's decided a summer wedding on the coast would be more fitting. I want this to be perfect for her. Special, ya know?" He paused waiting on a response from me.

I didn't respond.

"You still there?"

"Yes, Daddy, I'm listening."

"Oh, okay, good. This is going to cost a good bit more than originally planned. Also, family members who Shandra's grandmother insisted should attend are flying in from all over. The house is going to be packed."

Still not sure what it was he wanted to tell me other than

his wedding plans, which I did not think were a very urgent matter, I waited.

"There just isn't room for you at the house. I can't very well make Shandra's grandmother give you a room when she's being so generous already. Plus, the cost of travel is really making my budget tight. Flying you out and paying for your hotel room just isn't possible. I mean, I want you there, but I just don't see how I can afford to get you there."

I leaned back against the wall and closed my eyes. Tears welled up in my eyes, and I wiped at them furiously. I would not cry over this. I would not.

"Okay. All right," I managed through my clogged throat.

"So you understand, right?"

He was spending all his money on a wedding with a girl he was about to start a brand-new family with. He couldn't manage to find money to fly the daughter he already had out to be with him for his big day. As much as it hurt, this was something I could live with. I knew, though, the reality of what he was telling me was so much more.

A new wife, a new house, a big wedding, a new baby . . . My dad wasn't going to help me with college. I didn't even have the courage to ask anymore. If I had to be disappointed and let down by him one more time, I wasn't sure I could deal.

"Lana?"

"Yeah, okay, Daddy. I understand."

"I knew you would. Shandra is very worried this will upset you. I told her you were nothing like Caroline, and this wouldn't be a big deal for you."

"I need to go. I don't want to use up all my battery."

"Right, of course. Well, have fun and enjoy your summer. Maybe I can make it out to see you this fall. Which college did you finally decide on?"

I'd be going to the local junior college. My dad had a new family.

"I gotta go, Daddy," I replied, and clicked end.

The tears trickled down my face, and I felt my hardened resolve not to let my dad or my mother hurt me anymore melt away. How much was I supposed to take before I crumbled? Holding all this in was eating me alive. I needed someone to listen to me, someone to hold me while I cried. I just needed someone to care about *me*—not themselves. For once I needed it to be about me. . . . I needed Sawyer. I splashed water on my face and dried off all the tears. I didn't want to answer any questions on my way to find him. He was the only one I wanted to talk to about this.

Grabbing my bag, I tucked my phone inside and headed out the door. He'd be waiting on me. He'd listen. Just as I stepped onto the path leading down to our campsite, Sawyer came barreling toward me. Relief washed over me the moment I saw him. But it was short-lived. The serious expression on his face surprised me.

"Sawyer—" I began, but he rushed past me toward the bathhouse.

"I don't have time right now, Lana," he called back at me.

Stunned, I stood there frozen in my spot.

Within seconds he was running back out of the bathhouse with a dripping wet rag in his hand and a determined set to his jaw. His eyes flicked past me. As he rushed by, I reached out and grabbed his arm. He was starting to scare me.

"What's wrong?" I asked.

"Lana, let go. I can't talk to you right now. Ash needs me."

As his words registered in my head, I snatched my hand away from him. He didn't offer an explanation or apology. Instead he ran off, leaving me standing there alone. My emotions were already in tatters, so I tried to reason that something must really be wrong with Ashton. Panic sent me running after him.

I stopped the moment I saw Sawyer bend down behind Ashton and gently pull her hair back. She was sick. Sawyer wiped her mouth then folded the rag carefully and began washing her pale face.

"I got you, Ash. It's okay," he murmured as she laid her head against his chest weakly.

Jealousy washed over me like a tidal wave, even though I knew she was sick. I didn't like seeing him so sweet and protective of her. Taking a step forward, I asked, "Ash, you okay?"

Sawyer's head snapped up, but I didn't meet his gaze. I wasn't sure I could. Ashton raised her head and let out a sigh. "I've got a migraine. Too much sun, but Beau took the car to the nearest store to get me some pain medicine."

"Can I do anything?" I asked.

"I've got her, Lana. You can go on to the tent." Sawyer's demanding voice sliced through my already-broken spirit. I couldn't stand here and watch this. Ash was sick, but she was in good hands. The Vincent boys were taking care of her.

"Okay," I managed to respond, and turned to walk toward the tent. Standing outside of it, I hated the idea of going inside. The memories from last night were in there. I needed to forget those memories. My life was out of control enough. I didn't need Sawyer Vincent's help to break my heart. My dad was doing a fine job all on his own. I'd loved two men in my life, and I'd not been enough for either of them. I would never be their first choice.

A fresh tear rolled down my face. Before anyone could see me cry, I opened the tent and crawled inside. Moving my sleeping bag back to the far corner of the tent—as far away from Sawyer's as possible—I curled up inside of it and cried. I cried because my dad hadn't wanted me. I cried because my dreams of college had slipped through my fingers. And I cried because I'd let myself believe Sawyer could possibly fall in love with me.

*　　*　　*

I woke up early and peeked over at Sawyer. He was sound asleep in his sleeping bag. The pain he'd inflicted last night hadn't eased with sleep. Grabbing my things, I quietly exited the tent. I didn't want to be in there with him when he woke up.

"You're up early." Jake knelt down over the fire, adding some fresh logs.

Running my hand through my hair self-consciously, I nodded.

"I have coffee. Want some?" Jake asked, standing up and lifting a pot of coffee to show me.

"How did you make that?" I asked, walking over toward him. I could smell the coffee.

"I brought a coffeemaker with me. I used the electricity up at the bathhouse," he explained, pouring some of it into a Styrofoam cup.

"You'll have to drink it black. I don't have cream or sugar," he said, holding the cup out for me.

"I always drink it black," I replied, taking a small sip.

Jake raised his eyebrows. "Really? That's hot."

Rolling my eyes, I turned to walk up to the bathhouse and get dressed.

"What? I don't get a thank-you?"

I glanced back over my shoulder. "Thank you."

He smirked and shook his head.

"You know, it'll always be that way. He'll never really move on. She'll always be the one."

I stopped and took a deep breath as the knife he'd plunged into my stomach and twisted caused too much pain to keep me moving.

"I'm not being mean. I'm just being honest. You're wasting your time."

I nodded sharply; I forced my feet to move. I needed to get away. No more truth. I'd had a little too much of that in the past twelve hours. I needed a break.

Chapter 16

SAWYER

I'd royally screwed up. Old habits die hard, and my need to help Ash and protect her was a very old habit. Last night when Beau had left me with her, asking me to take care of her while he went to get the pain meds, I'd taken one look at her pale face and panicked. I'd needed to be the one to ease her pain. It just flipped a switch in me.

When Beau had returned and she'd curled up in his arms as he rocked her and soothed her, the reality of the situation washed over me. I'd been a stand-in. She'd not clung to me that way. She never would again. She was Beau's.

Opening the tent and seeing Lana curled up as far away from my sleeping bag as she could get told me all I needed to know. She'd seen what I hadn't last night until it was too late. Only twenty-four hours before, I'd been touching and kissing

her body in places that had given us both our first real experience with pleasure. I'd been so tempted to reach for her and
pull her against me as she slept, but I knew my touch wouldn't
be welcome. I'd been abrupt and rude to her when she'd
inquired about Ashton. Looking back, I knew I'd not wanted
her to see me taking care of Ashton. I wanted her to go away
so she wouldn't see me treating Ash with a tenderness no one
else had ever brought out in me. This was my secret moment
with Ash, my step back in time when she'd turned into my
arms. Lana being there had caused things in me to stir, things
I didn't understand. With Lana standing there wide-eyed and
hurt, it made what was happening wrong. It screwed with my
head.

She'd been gone from the tent when I woke up, and she'd
ignored me ever since. I didn't know what to say to her. How
did I explain last night? How did I make that better? Since
we started our hike this morning, she had been leading the
group like a woman intent on getting away. I didn't catch up
to her. She'd refused to make eye contact with me over break-
fast, and I was too much of a chicken-shit to force her to
acknowledge me.

"Why couldn't I have stayed back at the campsite with
Ash and Beau?" Heidi whined behind me.

"Because Ash is recovering from her migraine last night,
and Beau is taking care of her. Trust me, they want privacy.

At least, I know Beau does." Jake chuckled.

"She's sick, Jake. She isn't going to screw Beau on the hard ground in a tent," Heidi hissed.

"Who said she was gonna be the one on the ground?" Jake replied.

Listening to talk about Beau and Ash's sex life wasn't something I was in the mood for. I quickened my pace until I was only steps behind Lana. The little shorts she was wearing cupped her ass tightly as she took each long stride.

I'd had my hand on that sweet little bottom just the other night, but I was having my doubts that I'd ever get that chance again. The idea bothered me. No, I wasn't okay with that. I wasn't ready to let her go. August wasn't here yet. I wasn't ready to walk away from her.

"Are you going to ever speak to me again?" I asked.

She paused before continuing her uphill trek. "Sure. What do you want to talk about?" she replied in a bored voice.

"Lana, please slow down and talk to me," I pleaded.

She didn't slow down. If anything, she picked up her speed. If she kept this up, she was going to have to break into a run.

"Nothing to talk about, Sawyer. I'd rather just walk."

Reaching out, I grabbed her hand and stopped her. She tried snatching it back, but I held firm.

"Let go of me," she said with a snarl, finally lifting those bright green eyes to meet mine. The hurt in them made my knees weak. *Ah, damn. What the hell had I done?*

"Please, Lana, please talk to me," I begged, closing the distance between us.

"Keep walking, folks. Nothing to see. Let Sawyer attempt to clean up the mess he's made," Jake announced as the others walked past us.

Once they'd gotten far enough ahead, I let Lana pull her hand free of my grasp.

"Fine. Talk," she said, crossing her arms protectively over her chest.

"Last night—" I began trying to think of how I could explain this to her without making it worse.

"I'll help you since you seem to have lost your words," she interrupted. "Last night Ashton got sick, and you had an excuse to hold her and take care of her. You went into protect-and-comfort-Ashton mode. Nothing or no one else mattered because you love her. She needed you, and you were right there for her without question. You wouldn't let me help her because you couldn't stand the thought of missing the chance to hold her."

"That's not it. Being tuned into helping Ashton is a habit. I've been doing it for most of my life. That kind of habit is hard to break."

Lana let out a hard laugh. "Really? Well, isn't that a cute, little tidy way to wrap up everything I just said?" Lana took a step toward me, pointed a finger at my chest, and jabbed me with it. "I'm tired of being second choice or third choice. I've got enough of that in my life. Last night, I needed someone too. I needed someone to listen to me. Too bad no one wants to be Lana's shoulder to cry on. No one cares that Lana needs someone to give a crap about her." Her eyes glistened with unshed tears, and my chest got so tight I felt like it was about to crack open. "This is over. Leave it alone. I'm done," Lana spat, then turned around and began to walk away.

Acting quickly, I reached out and wrapped my hand around her arm. "What happened last night? Why did you need me?"

Her shoulders heaved, and I pulled her back against my chest and held her whether she wanted me to or not.

"Let me go, Sawyer." Her voice broke.

"No. Now tell me what you meant by all that."

Another sob broke free and she shook her head angrily. "*No.* You don't get to demand answers. I don't tell people much. I keep my emotions inside. But last night I wanted to tell *you.*" She let out a short, sad laugh. "I thought I might have had someone who wanted to listen—someone who would care. But I was wrong."

"No, you weren't. I do care. I want you to talk to me."

"Too late," she said with a growl, pulling against the hold I had on her.

"I was wrong last night, Lana. I'm so sorry. Please forgive me. Please, please forgive me. It'll never happen again." I paused, unsure if I was ready to bare my soul to her.

"You're right. It won't happen again. Because I'm done with trying to make people care about me. I shouldn't have to work so hard to get those who I love to love me back. No one else has to try so damn hard. No one. Just me. Just Lana McDaniel. I've had it. If I am so difficult to want, then I don't need anyone. I've managed alone this far. I'm a freaking pro!"

If it were possible for someone else's pain to break your heart, then Lana's pain had just shattered mine. Emotion burned my throat as I tightened my hold on her. I'd wanted to get inside her head. She was so closed off, and I'd wondered why. Then I knew. She didn't trust anyone enough to let them in—until last night. She'd decided she could let me in, and what had I done? I'd thrown her trust in her face. God, I was the world's biggest idiot.

"I'm so sorry," I whispered, pressing a kiss to her temple. "Can you forgive me? Can you trust me to put you first? I swear what happened last night will never happen again. It was the first time I'd had to deal with something like that since the break-up. When Beau came back and Ashton scrambled into his lap and arms with desperation to be near him, it didn't hurt the way I thought it would. It just slapped some sense into me. She didn't need me anymore. She wasn't mine to protect. I could move on. It was time. Last night was the closure I needed." I stopped and grabbed Lana's shoulders, turning her around to face me. Her red, swollen eyes just about sent me to my knees. "This is new for me. I'm learning how to have a relationship with someone other than Ashton. I made a horrible mistake. It was like a relapse. But you"—I reached up and tucked the tear dampened hair that had worked its way loose behind her ear—"you touch a place inside of me that Ashton never did. I feel things with you I never felt for her. I loved her for a very long time. I can't help the fact I still want to be there if she needs me. Next time there is a choice to make, it will be you I choose first. I can promise you that."

Lana searched my face as if she was waiting for more. I wasn't sure what else I could say.

"It isn't easy always being second best," she said. "Soon I'll be third best with my dad. I keep getting pushed down the list with him. Maybe that makes me selfish, but I just need there to be someone who I can run to. Last night I was running to you." She paused and swallowed. "You would think, after the rejection I've been dealt in my life, that I'd be used to it. But it doesn't get easier. Not really. It makes you cautious. It makes you careful not to get your hopes up. I got my hopes up with you. It'll be hard for me to hand that kind of trust over again. This doesn't mean we can't still see each other this summer. It just means we need to take a few steps back. We sped forward the other night in the tent. Now we need to back up."

She was forgiving me. I could earn her trust again. She'd open up to me again, and I'd be ready for it. I would be there when she needed me.

"Fair enough," I replied. I slipped a finger under her chin and tilted her head back. "I need to kiss you now."

"Okay," she whispered as my lips touched hers.

LANA

Beau had the camp packed up and strapped down on top of the Suburban when we arrived back at the campsite. He said Ashton needed to sleep in a decent bed tonight and we were all going to go to a hotel, then head home in the morning. No one argued with him. I think we all were ready for a real bed anyway. I almost sighed in relief.

I told Jake to sit up front with Sawyer and I said I'd sit in the back beside Ashton. I just wasn't ready to spend any more time with Sawyer right now. I'd forgiven him, but my heart was still wounded. Ashton had understood, and she'd reached down and held my hand as I slid in beside her. It had been a quiet trip.

We were at the closest affordable hotel, and the guys were getting our rooms. I wasn't sure if I was sharing a room with Sawyer or if I was expected to get my own. I had enough to get my own if I needed to. There was no reason to save up for my college dreams. My dad had shot those hopes down.

Sitting in the lobby of the hotel, I waited with the other girls. I was still dirty from our day outdoors, and I wanted a shower, not to mention I was exhausted physically and emotionally.

Sawyer walked toward me with his backpack and mine slung over his shoulders. "You need to get anything out of that duffel bag you and Ash are sharing?"

"Um . . . yeah. I guess. Are we sharing a room?"

Sawyer looked concerned as he closed the short distance between us. "I thought we were okay. You didn't sit beside me, but I figured you wanted to check on Ash."

"That's fine. I was just wondering. I can get my own room if needed."

Sawyer reached out and slipped his hand in mine. I let him thread his fingers through mine. "I want you with me."

I nodded and forced a smile. He bent down and kissed me on the forehead. "I'm going to fix this. I promise you. You'll trust me again," he whispered before straightening back up and leading me toward the elevator.

*   *   *

We all managed to get rooms on the same floor. Sawyer slipped the key card into the door to room 314 and opened it up. He held out his hand for me to enter first. The room was roomier than most hotels I'd stayed at, but then he'd been determined that we were staying at the Marriott instead of the mom-and-pop motel across the street. A king-size bed sat in the center of everything.

"One bed," I said, glancing back at him.

"They didn't have any doubles available. Is this okay?"

"Sure," I replied, and reached for my backpack still on his shoulder. "Can I take a shower first?"

He slid my backpack down his arm and handed it to me. "Of course. Take your time. I'll order us some dinner."

"Okay, thank you."

I turned to walk into the bathroom.

"Lana?" His voice sounded sad. I hated making him sad, but I didn't have the energy to do anything about it. I was drained.

"Yes?" I asked, and turned to look back at him. He reminded me of a lost little boy. His perfect face was troubled.

"I'm sorry."

"For what?"

"Being an idiot," he replied.

"I've already forgiven you, Sawyer."

179

He looked defeated. "Have you really?"

"My forgiving you doesn't make my heart hurt less. It takes a while to heal."

I didn't wait for his response. I closed the door behind me and turned on the shower.

Chapter 17

LANA

Sunlight poured in through the window, and an arm held me tightly while a leg had me pinned to the bed. Sawyer had snuggled up against my back at some point the night before. I'd eaten the cheeseburger he'd ordered me, as well as few bites of chocolate cake before curling up as far away from his side of the bed as possible and falling asleep instantly. I was still on my side, but Sawyer was pressed up against me. He was holding on to me like I was some sort of lifeline.

I reached up to move his arm so I could get up and go use the bathroom.

"Don't. Please, just let me hold you a little bit longer," he mumbled into my hair.

"You're awake," I replied.

"Mmhmm, and I'm enjoying myself. Please, just a little bit longer."

I smiled for the first time since the Ashton incident.

"You can still enjoy yourself without me," I teased.

He froze for a second before snuggling even closer to me and moving his hand so that his palm covered my bare stomach where my tank top had inched up in my sleep.

"I can't enjoy it without you. You're what I'm enjoying," he whispered in a deep, sleepy voice as he took a small nip at my earlobe.

"Ah!" I squealed, and he chuckled, sending chill bumps over my arms from the warmth of his breath, tickling my ear and neck.

"I missed you so much," he replied in a more serious tone.

I didn't need to point out that I'd been with him for three days. I knew what he meant. Mentally and emotionally, I'd been checked out yesterday. My chest didn't ache this morning, and I could breathe deeply again. Maybe it was the fact Sawyer's big arms were wrapped around me, giving me a false sense of safety.

"Can I go to the restroom, please?" I asked, tickling his arm with my nails.

"Will you promise to come back?"

I had planned on jumping in the shower again and getting ready. However, as much as I hated to admit it, I'd missed him, too.

"Yes, if that's what you want."

"I want," he murmured in my ear, and pressed a soft kiss to my temple.

SAWYER

"Bring the small bottle of mouthwash with you," I called out when I heard the bathroom door open.

Lana walked around the bed and handed me the bottle. "Here ya go."

I opened it and took a swig then swished it around some before swallowing it.

"You did not just swallow that!"

Grinning, I reached up and grabbed her tiny waist, pulling her down on top of me.

"I believe I did. I probably need mouth-to-mouth to save me from the poisoning," I teased, leaning up and taking a nip at her bottom lip.

"Mouth-to-mouth won't save you from poisoning. You need your stomach pumped," she informed me as she pressed a kiss to the side of my mouth.

"Hmmmm . . . well, that sounds like a lot of work. I'll think about it later." I slipped my hands into her messy curls and brought her mouth down to mine. Just as Lana opened her mouth to let me inside, her phone started singing.

She pulled back from the kiss. I needed this kiss. I needed reassurance I hadn't lost this . . . whatever it was we had between us. "Don't answer it," I begged, reaching up to kiss her chin. Laughing softly, she curled back into my arms and let me get a taste of her minty, toothpaste-flavored mouth. But the minute the ringing stopped, it started up again. Lana lifted her head, frowned, and glanced over at her phone. I fought the urge to grab the phone and throw it against the wall to shut it up.

"It might be an emergency," she said, and I loosened my hold on her and let her crawl off me to check her phone. The tense expression that came over her face had me sitting up and checking to see who was bothering her—because it obviously wasn't a welcome call.

MOM flashed across the screen.

Lana slipped out of bed. "I need to take this. She'll just keep calling until I do."

"Hello, Mom." Her voice sounded tired instead of worried by her mother's determination to get her on the phone. Lana walked around the bed and headed for the bathroom. Once the door clicked into place, I threw the pillow across the room and muttered a curse. She wouldn't be shutting me out if I'd been there for her. I was willing to bet she'd been going to tell me what crap her parents were putting her though the other night. I wouldn't have to worry now about how to fix it; I'd know what needed to be done.

"No, *Mom!*" I heard her raised voice, and I jumped out of bed to go listen at the door. I was invading her privacy, but she was upset. I had my reasons. It was a damn-good reason.

"I don't want you to call him. I don't want you to ask him. He's moved on, Mom. He's getting himself a brand-new family now, and we are his past. Just let this go. I'll figure this all out. Just leave it alone. Please."

Was she talking about her Dad?

"Mom, I'm an adult. You can't continue to try to make all my decisions for me. I get to make those now. So please, back off."

I walked away from the door and walked over to the window overlooking the mountains we'd left last night. Why did I care so much about finding out her problems? It wasn't like we were an actual couple. I tensed up as that realization came over me. I had no claim on Lana. If Ethan or anyone else asked her out again, I couldn't stop her from saying yes. Someone else could touch the soft, smooth skin on her arms, her thighs, her stomach, her . . . oh, hell no. I needed to fix this and fast. This was more than a fling now. Sure, we were going our separate ways in August, but right then, I didn't want to share. I wouldn't be able to share. I was pretty damn sure I'd rip another guy's arms off his body if I saw him touch her.

The bathroom door opened, and Lana stepped out. A forced smile touched her lips as her eyes met mine.

"Everything okay?" I asked, hoping to God that she'd tell me what was going on in her life.

Instead she only shrugged. Damn it.

"Lana, listen, we need to talk about something . . . ," I began, walking across the room so I could touch her and in case I needed to beg.

She shook her head. "If this is bad news, I really don't think I can handle that right now. Give me a few hours first, please."

Well, hell, if the pain in her voice didn't rip me in two. I pulled her against my chest and held her there. She was stiff as a board at first, but I continued to rub her back and kiss the top of her head until she relaxed and wrapped her arms around my waist.

"It isn't bad. But it is time sensitive," I explained.

She tilted her head to look at me. "Time sensitive?"

"Very. As in someone could lose a limb if they stepped out of line."

Lana pulled back, and the frown puckering her brow was adorable. "What in the world are you talking about, Sawyer?"

"The fact I want—no, I need—for us to be exclusive until we part ways when we head off to college."

Lana made a small *O* with her mouth, and then she nodded slowly. "Okay. That sounds like a good plan. But why would someone lose a limb?"

I traced her bottom lip with my finger. "Because if they touched you, I'd have to rip off the offending limb."

A small bubble of laughter escaped her and she bit down on my finger. Her eyes smiled up at me like a playful kitten.

"So you want to play rough, do you?" I picked her up and threw her down on the bed before covering her body with mine.

LANA

The ride back to Grove went fast, but then I'd slept most of the way. Jake had not been happy when Sawyer informed him that I was sitting up front. I felt bad about it, but I liked knowing Sawyer wanted me close to him.

Everyone had loaded their gear into their cars and left. Ashton had even gone inside to go to bed. She was still pretty weak. Sawyer took my bags and put them inside the door of the house, then looked back at me.

"Come with me for a while," he said, pulling me back outside onto the porch and closing the door behind me.

"You aren't tired from all that driving?"

He shook his head and pulled me up against him. My aunt and uncle weren't home, but they could drive up at any minute. I wasn't sure what they'd think of this.

"Okay. Let me go check on Ash, and I'll be right back down."

"I'll wait here," he replied, letting go of my hand so I could run back inside.

I knocked softly on Ashton's door, then peeked my head inside. She was already curled up under the covers. Closing her door softly, I headed back to Sawyer.

"She okay?" he asked as I stepped outside.

"Yep."

"Good. Let's go."

He rested his hand on my lower back and led me toward the

Suburban. "First things first, I've got to go get my truck from the house. I want you to be able to sit close enough to me so that I can touch you if I want to."

Smiling to myself, I climbed inside.

I'd been to Sawyer's house with Ashton before. We were younger, and I never went inside. We mostly just swam in the lake back behind his property. Walking in the front door with my hand clasped firmly in his was a little nerve-racking. His parents weren't home, and he'd convinced me to come inside.

"This way." He motioned for me to go ahead of him down a staircase leading to what looked like the basement.

"Why are we going down here?" I asked, peering back at him over my shoulder.

"This is my cave. Go on," he encouraged me.

His cave . . . hmm. I walked the rest of the way down the stairs and stopped at the bottom, unsure which door to open. There were two: one on my right and one on my left. Sawyer reached over me and twisted the knob on the right door, then reached in and flipped a switch. The lights came on, and I stood there in wonder as I took in the room.

It was huge. Two large, black leather sectional sofas sat in the middle of the room in front of a massive flat-screen television that hung on the wall. A crimson refrigerator with the University of Alabama's logo on the outside sat against the left side of the room, and a black marble countertop, complete with a sink, sat off to the left of the fridge. On the other wall, shelves and shelves full of trophies stretched from floor to ceiling. Framed football jerseys stood among the trophies. Under the television sat a long, black narrow table, complete with an Xbox and a Wii. Photos, all of them carefully framed, also cluttered the surface. Sawyer's mother had to have done that. I couldn't imagine him actually framing photos to sit out.

"You thirsty?" he asked, walking over to the fridge and opening it. "Looks like Loretta came this week. It's stocked. Coke, Mountain Dew, blue Gatorade, or bottled water?"

"Loretta?" I asked, confused.

"The housekeeper. She does all the grocery-shopping, too."

"Oh." People actually had housekeepers that did their grocery shopping? How odd.

"Um, water is fine." I walked over to the shelves and began reading the plaques on the trophies. MVP seemed to be the most popular award he had received.

"Here ya go." He handed me a water and turned his attention to the shelves. "Mom did all this. She wanted somewhere for all these to be displayed. She actually tried to turn one of the guest bedrooms into a "Sawyer Shrine," or so my father called it. He refused to let her and suggested she stick them down here. I agreed with him just so they would be somewhat hidden."

"There's a lot of them," I replied, taking a sip of the water.

"Yeah, there is." He nodded his head toward the couch. "Come, sit down with me. We can find us a movie to rent off iTunes."

I followed him to the end of one of the leather sectionals. He set his Gatorade down, reached up, took my water, and put it down beside his. "Come here." His voice dropped to that husky whisper that made my heart speed up. I let him pull me down onto his lap.

"I've been thinking about this mouth all day," he confided before covering my lips with his. I licked at his bottom lip, and he opened for me, letting me leisurely taste him. The gentle pressure of his mouth was perfect and made me a little dizzy.

His fingers slid up my thighs until both hands were cupping my butt. One of his fingers traced the edge of my panties. "I really like this skirt," he murmured against my lips. I really liked it too at the moment. My breath was coming in short gasps as he slid one hand inside the edge of my panties. He caressed my bare butt with one hand while he slid his other slowly back down my thigh and shifted closer to my inner thigh. I knew what his next move would be. What I didn't know was if I was going to let it go that far.

Then he moaned into my mouth as his fingers touched the inside of my thigh and my leg fell open of its own accord. The slow, easy kiss became frenzied as we both fought to calm our breathing. His hand inched higher and higher up my exposed thigh. The second his finger grazed the outside of my panties, I jerked in his hold, and something very close to pleading squeaked in my throat. Sawyer pulled back, and his accelerated breathing made me tingle with pleasure. I loved knowing I did this to him.

He kissed down my neck until he met the curve of my shoulder. He went very still. His warm breath bathed my chest and neck. His hand slowly moved again. One lone finger slipped inside the edge of my panties and made direct contact. He murmured something against my neck, but I couldn't focus enough to understand. My brain was in a foggy haze, and my heart was about to pound out of my chest. The urge to move against the hand, which now cupped the crotch of my panties, was strong. But I waited while he eased his finger farther inside and gently ran it along the folds.

"Oh, oh, oh, my god," I managed to get out in a breathless chant.

"God, you're so warm," he whispered in a strained voice as he began kissing the spot where he had buried his head in my neck.

When he slipped his other hand over my leg and pulled it farther open then reached down and pulled my panties to the side as he gently stroked me, I started to come apart in his arms.

"That's it, baby," he encouraged as I clung to him, calling his name and wanting it to never end.

When I could finally catch my breath, his fingers left me and pulled my panties back into place. Then I was being cuddled in his arms as he whispered things against my neck between kisses and little nibbles.

Sawyer finally lifted his head from the tender skin along my neck that he'd loved thoroughly. "That was ... That was ... damn," he whispered before claiming my mouth again. After a long leisurely kiss, Sawyer lay down on the couch and tucked me back against him. "Let's watch that movie now," he said in a teasing voice.

The minute Ashton pulled her Jetta into the clearing down by the Vincent's lake Sawyer came jogging toward us. His hair was slicked back and wet, with droplets of water flying off the thick locks. The navy blue swim trunks he was wearing hung on his waist and showcased his delicious abs and hip bones.

"Pretty sure he isn't running out here to see me," Ashton quipped as I sat there staring at him in awe.

Snapping myself out of my worshipful gaze, I opened the car door and stepped out. Sawyer was instantly beside me.

"I didn't think you'd ever get here," he said in a pleased voice as his cold wet hand clasped mine and pulled me up against his chest. He was getting my dry clothes damp, but I wasn't going to complain.

"Sorry, we overslept," I explained.

"Don't apologize to him. He was the one who kept you out late," Ashton teased, and headed off in the direction of Beau as he made his way toward her.

"I had a good time last night," Sawyer informed me in a husky whisper.

We'd gone to get something to eat at Hank's, then gone out to the field. There was no party last night. Sawyer took advantage of the location and brought a large blanket for us, and we lay on our backs under the stars. I pointed out different constellations, and he tried to get his hands under different parts of my clothing while pretending to listen to me. It had been perfect.

"I did too," I replied, smiling up at him.

He lowered his head to kiss me softly then whispered, "Let's go see if I can't teach you how to do a flip off that rope swing."

Shaking my head, I stifled a giggle. "No way. You tried that once, and I ended up with ten stitches in my head."

Sawyer rubbed his hand gently over the back of my head. I'd sliced it open on a rock; I was ten and I'd panicked. When Sawyer had said, "Let go of the rope—*now*," it had taken me a few seconds to obey. Those few seconds were the difference between me landing in the deep water and me landing on the edge of the shore. I never tried that swing again.

"I promise I won't let you get hurt this time. Besides, I was like ten. I sucked at teaching people things. I'm so much better now." He squeezed my hand and brought it to his lips before leading me out toward the lake.

Laughter and squealing traveled loud and clear across the water. At least twenty or so people were already there. It was supposed to have been the last party at the lake before everyone went off to college. I'd never been down here with more than just Sawyer, Ashton, and Beau. Girls were lying out on the pier, guys were climbing the tree to do dangerous tricks off the rope swing, and not one person had a beer in their hands. It was a miracle.

"You're really not going to go on that rope with me?" Sawyer asked. "I'll hold the rope; you hold me. And no flips."

"You promise no flips?" I asked him, watching his face for any sign of a fib.

"Promise," he assured me, reaching for the hem of my shirt and pulling it off.

He stopped and held it in his hand, staring at the bikini I'd bought only because Jewel begged me to. It wasn't something I'd normally wear, but I figured if I was coming to Sawyer Vincent's lake party as his date, I needed to be able to keep his attention as the other bikini-clad girls ran around. Especially Ashton. When I'd seen the red bikini she'd laid out to wear, I knew I had to step up my game.

"Uh, would you consider putting this shirt back on?" he asked me as he started to put it back over my head.

I reached up and stopped him. "No, *Sawyer*, stop."

He stepped in closer and frowned down at me. "There isn't a lot to this swimsuit, Lana."

I glanced around and took note of all the other swimsuits girls were wearing. Mine was not even one of the skimpiest. Turning my attention back to him, I took the shirt out of his hand.

"It's called a bikini, Sawyer. If you look around, you'll notice a lot of them. We girls tend to wear them when we swim." My voice dripped with sarcasm.

"I'm aware of that, Lana, but I don't like the idea of everyone seeing so much of you. This thing barely covers up your boobs. I'm scared to see how much of your sexy ass it shows off."

Oh. He was jealous.

"My bottom is covered." I turned around and shimmied out of my cut-off blue jean shorts, my butt facing in his direction.

"Ah, hell," he said with a groan, and reached out and pulled me back toward him. "Could you at least not do that little booty shaking thing with little pieces of fabric being your only cover?"

I couldn't help it. I laughed.

"You think this is funny?" he whispered, resting his hands on my waist.

"I think it's hilarious," I replied, turning around to press a kiss on his pouty lips. He really was very unhappy about this bikini. "Come on, I thought we were going to do the rope swing."

His frown deepened. "I don't know if that's a good idea. One of those tiny strips of material may fall off on impact."

Rolling my eyes, I reached for his hand and pulled him toward the tree. "You're being ridiculous, Sawyer. Come on."

Muttering under his breath, he followed me to the tree. He went behind me, his hands on my bottom. I wasn't sure if he was helping me up or trying to cover me up. Either way, it was cute.

Once we made our way out onto the limb, a guy I didn't know threw the rope back toward Sawyer and I realized I might have spoken too soon. It was terrifying from up here.

"Don't look down," Sawyer directed as he held on to my waist and moved in front of me so he could grab the rope. He squatted down. "Steady yourself by holding on to my shoulders. Then wrap your legs around my waist."

I studied his back and wondered if it would be that big of a deal if I just went back down the tree the dry way.

Sawyer glanced back at me. "Come on, Lana. I got this. You'll be fine."

I wasn't so sure about the "fine" part, but I gave in and did as instructed.

Sawyer stood up. I wrapped my arms around his neck and closed my eyes.

"Take one of your arms and put it under mine. If you do it this way, you're going to choke me to death," he instructed with an amused tone.

I hadn't thought of that. I guessed that it might be a bad idea. I gripped his shoulder tightly with one hand as I slid the other one under his arm. I stretched both my arms until I could clench my hands and tighten my hold on Sawyer's body.

"Perfect. Now hold on, baby, 'cause here we go." On his last word, we were airborne.

I opened my eyes just in time to see him let go of the rope, and I closed them back again, squealing as we plummeted toward the water.

The lake water wasn't as cold as I'd expected when we dropped down into it. I was extremely grateful. I released Sawyer and kicked my legs, pushing my way back toward the surface. It was then that I noticed my bottoms had slipped down underneath my butt. Reaching down and tugging them up, I was glad Sawyer wouldn't know he'd been partially right about my swimsuit coming off during impact.

Sawyer's head emerged a few seconds after mine, and he was grinning like an idiot.

"What?" I asked.

He winked as he reached over and pulled me up against him. "I can see real good under this water," he murmured, and understanding dawned on me.

I slapped him on the arm. He laughed, then dropped a quick kiss on my lips.

"Wanna go again?" he asked with a smirk.

Chapter 18

SAWYER

After a week of dates with Lana—either at my house, at the field party, or at Hank's—it was time I took her somewhere nice. She never complained and was open to anything I suggested. Even the other day, when I'd asked if she'd wanted to go with me to pick out stuff for my dorm room, she'd happily gone with me. Granted, I had to rein her in on her decorating ideas. I was a guy, and my curtains and quilts didn't need to match. I just needed something dark enough to block out the sun on mornings I might actually get to sleep in.

That day I'd decided to surprise her with a trip to New Orleans. It was a two-hour drive from Grove. The only info I'd given her was that she needed to wear a sundress and comfortable shoes. The restaurant I was taking her to that night was too nice for shorts and required a little bit of a dressier look. We'd be doing a good amount of walking the streets, too. As much as I loved her legs in heels, I didn't figure she'd thank me for not warning her about the walking.

I couldn't think of a time I'd been this anxious to see someone. She'd fallen asleep in my arms last night, and I'd had to sneak out the window in Ashton's room that Beau had used many times when we were kids.

I pressed the button on the garage door opener and started to back out when my eyes landed on Ashton standing in front of her Jetta directly behind me. Opening my truck door, I stepped out and walked out to where she was standing.

Tears were streaming down her face and her shoulders were shaking with loud sobs. *What the hell?*

"Ash, what's wrong? Is Lana okay?" My heart constricted. Why else would Ash be in my driveway crying like someone was dead? *God, please tell me Lana is okay.* I'd just left her in her bed a few hours ago. She'd been fine.

"Ash, tell me what's wrong *now*." I felt my throat tighten up, and I resisted the urge to grab her shoulders and shake her. I needed her to speak.

"Lana is fine." She sobbed, and I took a deep gulp of air as my panic eased off. This wasn't about Lana. I could calm down.

"Thank God," I said breathlessly.

"It's Beau—He . . . He . . ." She burst into tears again.

"Is Beau okay?" I asked, and she shoved Beau's cell phone into my hands.

"Just read that text," she said, wailing.

Read what text? Shaking my head, I looked down at Beau's phone. The text that had Ashton all upset was already opened on the screen.

> Sugar: Hey sexy. I had a blast dancing with you last week. And you owe me one more game of pool. That was an unfair game, and you know it. You distracted me. So you find another night away from that ball and chain of yours and get your gorgeous ass back to the bar next weekend when I'm back in town. XOXO.

I lifted my eyes to meet Ashton's red swollen ones, and all I could think about was exactly how I was going to murder my brother.

LANA

> Sawyer: I can't make it. Not sure if you've talked to Ash, but Beau cheated on her and she needs me. I've got to go beat his sorry ass

and then see what I can do to calm her down. She was outside on my driveway this morning bawling her eyes out.

I reread the text message from Sawyer for the third time before I finally put my phone down. I don't know what surprised me more: Beau cheating on Ash or Sawyer dropping me to fix her problems. He could have at least called me. Maybe asked for my help with Ash. He'd done neither, because this was what he'd been waiting on. All this time, I was just a fill-in while he waited. Beau served Ashton up to him on a silver platter, and I wasn't stupid enough to think I stood a chance of holding on to him. He loved her. He just liked me. I was the summer fling. She was the girl he wanted to spend forever with.

Picking my phone back up, I found Jewel's number and pressed send.

"It's about time you called me. How's it going with Mr. Hot and Sexy?"

"It's not. I need to leave. Can I come there?"

"Uh-oh. That doesn't sound good. Of course, you can come here. Do I need to come get you? Because it could be like tonight before I get there. I have plans with this fabulously hot lifeguard. He has the best ass I've ever seen. His hair is a little long, but I can overlook that."

"No, I'll get a ride. I'll see you in a few hours. Thanks, Jewel."

"No problemo, chica. See ya soon."

I hung up the phone and dialed one more number.

"Hello?" The cautious tone in Ethan's voice told me he knew who was calling.

"Hey, Ethan. It's Lana, and I have a huge favor to ask, but I'll pay you."

"Uh, okay—"

"I need a ride to the beach."

Ethan pulled into the parking lot near the condos where Jewel was staying. Her car was parked over to the left side of the building, so I knew we'd found the right place.

"I know you said you didn't want to talk about it, but I need to know *something*, Lana. Sawyer is going to lose it when he finds out you're gone, and he's my friend."

Cringing at the predicament I'd put Ethan in, I reached into my purse and pulled out five twenty dollar bills and handed it to him.

"I don't want your money. Just some kind of explanation."

"Beau and Ash are no longer, and Sawyer is busy comforting her and helping her nurse her broken heart. That's all you need to know."

Ethan frowned. "Are you sure about that? I can't think of any female who could ever turn Beau Vincent's head from Ash. He's been in love with her since we were kids."

"Well, believe it. Guess he got his fill and moved on. Luckily, she has the other Vincent boy in love with her to pick up the pieces. If she is smart, she'll grab hold of Sawyer and not let go. His love for her is unbreakable and unconditional."

"I've seen you and Sawyer at the field and out in town. He seemed completely over Ash to me. He watched you with such a predatory gleam in his eyes; I was scared to speak to you."

My heart broke a little more, and I forced the pain away. I would not do this. Sawyer Vincent would not break me. I was stronger than this. "Well, looks can be deceiving. I don't want to talk about this, Ethan. Please, just take the money so I don't have to feel guilty about asking you to drive me all the way out here after how things went down with you and me. I hate I was so blinded by Sawyer that I didn't give you a chance. I learned a lesson."

Ethan took the money I was thrusting at him. "I'll accept it if that's what is going to make you feel better, but I don't want to take the money."

I leaned over and pressed a kiss to his cheek. "Thank you for being there for me when I needed someone. You have no idea how rare that is for me."

I reached for the door handle and jumped down out of his Jeep. Reaching into the back, I started to grab my luggage when Ethan reached over me and picked up both suitcases. "I got them," he said before turning and heading for the condos.

"Which floor?" he asked as he stopped beside the elevators.

I followed behind him, carrying my cosmetics and toiletries bags. "Bottom, that one right there." I pointed to unit 103 just as the door swung open and Jewel stepped outside, squealing.

"You're here! You're here! Oh, and you brought one of the cuties from Wings with you."

"Good to see you again, Jewel," Ethan said politely, setting my luggage down outside the door and stepping back to let me pass.

"You too, uh—"

"Ethan. His name is Ethan."

"That's right." She snapped her fingers like it had been on the tip of her tongue.

"Well, Ethan, you want to come inside? We're having a party tonight. You're welcome to stay and crash."

Ethan glanced from Jewel to me and then shook his head. "Nah, I need to head out. I have plans tonight but thanks."

"Aw, phooey." Jewel pouted—it was so obviously fake. I wasn't sure why she attempted it, unless, of course, she thought it looked believable.

"Take care of yourself, Lana," Ethan said with a concerned expression.

"You too, Ethan. Thanks again." He nodded and headed back toward his Jeep.

* * *

Once he had gotten in his Jeep and had pulled out of the parking lot, Jewel grabbed my arm and tugged on it. "Come inside. Tell me all about Grove while I fix myself a sandwich."

I picked up my luggage and carried it inside. "Which room do you want me in?"

"Down the hall. It's the third door on the left. You have the best view of the ocean from that room. But don't lie on the bed yet. We need to strip that bed and wash the quilt and sheets. God only knows who's used that room during one of our parties."

Cringing, I made a mental note to go buy some Clorox spray and wipe the place down.

Chapter 19

SAWYER

As I banged on the door to Beau's trailer, I mentally cursed him. He'd had to have Ashton so damn bad he snatched her away from me, and for what? He'd lost her within seven months. How stupid could one man be?

"What the *hell* Sawyer?" Beau demanded as he opened the door and glared at me as if *he* had a reason to be mad.

I shoved past him and threw his phone down on the beat-up coffee table where I'd once sat and played Go Fish at two o'clock in the morning with Beau while waiting on his mom to get home from work.

"You better have a real good reason for this, Saw," he said with a growl, slamming the door behind him.

"Ash had your phone," I replied.

Beau looked down at his cell phone on the table and back to me. "So?"

The lack of concern was my first hint that we had a big misunderstanding on our hands.

"You got a text . . . from a girl," I continued, and waited for him to look worried or guilty or something.

He continued to look confused. The innocence of his lost expression told me all I needed to know. Beau hadn't cheated on Ash. Thank *God*. Maybe it wasn't too late for Lana and me to get to New Orleans today after all.

I picked up the phone and handed it to him. "Read the text from Sugar."

Then, as if a light went off, Beau's eyes widened, and my moment of relief was replaced by disbelief.

"Sugar texted me? And Ash read it?"

"Yes, you stupid ass-wipe. Haven't you learned by now that when you *cheat* you get *caught*? Damn it, Beau, how could you do this? She loves you. She's a complete mess. I found her on my carport bawling her eyes out this morning."

Beau's face went pale, and he grabbed a pair of discarded jeans, jerked them on, and turned to run out the door.

I followed him. "What the hell are you doing?"

"Where is she, Saw? Where's Ash?" he yelled as he ran to his truck.

"I'm not telling you where she is. You've destroyed her, Beau."

Beau stopped and stalked back toward me with an angry snarl on his face. "Sugar is my fucking *aunt*. My mother's baby sister. Now tell me where my girl is before I beat the shit out of you." His voice had gone from a cold menace to a roar.

"Since when do you have an aunt named Sugar? Aunt Honey's younger sister's name is Janet!" I yelled back. I wasn't sure what he was trying to do. I was his brother for crying out loud. I knew his family tree.

"Yeah, well, my mama's name is Paula, but that ain't the name she goes by, now is it?"

"Janet goes by Sugar?" I asked with relief.

"*Yes!* Now where the hell is my girl?"

I was pretty sure we'd woken up the entire trailer park. "She's at home. Go," I replied, and Beau turned and ran to his truck. It roared to life and he spun out of the driveway. I just hoped he didn't run over anyone on his way to her house because I was willing to bet he wasn't going to stop if he did.

Sinking down onto the steps, I pulled my phone out of my pocket and texted Ash.

Me: It isn't what it looks like. Beau is on his way over. Listen to him. Just so happens Aunt Honey has a younger sister; her name is Sugar. Tell Lana to get ready. I'm on my way there to get her.

Ashton: Oh, no. I made a mess of things. I'm
so sorry, Sawyer.
Me: Not that big of a deal. It got straightened
out pretty fast. Watch for Beau. He sped out of
here for your house like there was a fire.
Ashton: Okay.

I decided against sending Lana a text. I had a feeling I was probably in trouble because of the last text I'd sent. It hadn't explained
things well, but I had been in a hurry to find Beau and get Ashton
calmed down. Showing up and explaining was the best idea.

Beau met me at the door of Ashton's house when I got there.
The serious expression on his face surprised me. Surely, he'd been
able to clear things up with Ashton. Didn't she believe him?

"Hey, things okay?" I asked, walking up the steps.

"That depends on you," Beau replied.

"What?"

"Ash is upset but not with me. She's upset with herself. Running to you when she thought I'd cheated on her was her first reaction. It has always been the three of us. She didn't think about going
to anyone else. She just figured you would know how to fix it. You
always did fix the messes we managed to get into. I'm warning you
now that if you so much as blame, raise your voice, or even look
at her wrong when you walk in that house and hear what she has

to tell you, that I will take you down. She got upset. She acted on instinct. What happened as a repercussion isn't her fault."

"What in the hell are you getting at, Beau?" I asked, starting to feel anxious as I pushed past him and into the house. Ashton was standing in the kitchen, chewing on her bottom lip. Her eyes were swollen and red.

"What's wrong with the two of you?" I asked in confusion. "I'm just here for Lana. Whatever other problems y'all have, I'm out. Fix them yourselves."

"Oh, no. Oh, no. Oh, no," Ashton started muttering. Her worried eyes lifted to look at Beau for help.

"Just give it to him, Ash," Beau encouraged gently.

"Give me what?" I demanded. Then my eyes noticed the piece of paper dangling from her right hand.

I walked over to her and snatched the paper out of her grasp. Perfectly scripted handwriting covered the page in what appeared to be a letter. As I dropped my eyes to the bottom of the page, Lana's signature stood out at me and my heart stopped beating. *No, no, no, no, no, no. Please, God no,* I begged silently as I began reading.

Ashton,

Let me begin by saying thank you. I needed an escape this summer from the craziness that is my life. You helped make that possible. I needed to talk about my dad and how I felt, and you were there for me. No one has ever been there for me before. Knowing someone cared was more precious to me than you could have ever imagined.

But I made the mistake of opening my heart up to someone who clearly could never feel the same about me. I knew Sawyer loved you. I've known it since we were kids. I thought maybe just getting his attention for a short time would be enough. It wasn't.

I've grown up with two parents who never once thought about me in the choices they made. My emotions weren't something they concerned themselves with, and maybe that is my fault because I didn't speak up. I just pushed the hurt and anger deep inside me. I wanted to be strong because I knew they were weak. I'm tired of being strong. I'm tired of being second best. I need someone to love me.

Staying in Grove isn't a possible option for me. I let myself hope for too much. I've been broken too many times. I can't stay somewhere near . . . someone who will eventually destroy me.

Please tell your parents thank you for me. I'm sorry I didn't stick around for good-byes and explanations, but I think you understand why I had to go. You had the right Vincent boy all along. Don't take him for granted this time. He loves you in a way that I hope to one day inspire in someone. He would give up the world for you. When you have someone that special, that incredible who loves you, don't let it go. This is your second chance to treasure what you've had all your life. Sawyer was always the Vincent boy worth fighting for. He's the special one.

Love,

Lana

"She doesn't say where she went? Did she go home? How did she get there?" I was going to throw up. Tears stung my eyes, and I swallowed the lump in my throat. I didn't have time to cry like a damn baby. I needed to find Lana *immediately*.

Folding the paper neatly, I stuck it in my pocket and pulled out my phone. Her phone went straight to voice mail. *Shit*. "Did you try calling her? Have you called her mom?" I asked Ashton while trying her number again.

"Don't raise your voice at her," Beau said. "I know you're

upset, but remember my warning. And for the record, you're not all that damn special. Just throwing that out there."

I didn't give a rat's ass about Beau's warning. I needed to find Lana. "I'm not raising my voice. I need to find Lana!" I growled, glaring at him as I slammed my fist against the brick fireplace. The pain wasn't enough to numb the agony in my chest.

"Sawyer, stop! You're bleeding. Beau, do something." Ashton's worried voice sounded like it was coming down a tunnel.

"Where is she?" I roared, beating my fist against the wall, trying to stop the tears blurring my vision. I had to find her. She needed me. Oh, God, she needed me.

Pressing both my palms flat against the brick, I dropped my head and let the tears roll freely. I'd lost her. I couldn't lose her. She had been so broken, and I didn't even know. I wanted to find her dumbass father and beat his face in until the ache inside me, from her words in that letter, eased. How could they overlook her? How could anyone overlook her?

"Sawyer, we'll find her," Ashton said as a small, choked-up sob escaped her. "Beau, he's crying. I can't stand this. Do something," she begged.

"Why don't you give us a minute, Ash?" Beau replied.

I heard Beau whisper to Ashton and kiss her before her footsteps faded down the hall.

"Man, you've got to get a fucking grip. You're losing it,

and that shit ain't gonna help nothing. Plus you've got Ash in tears."

He had no right to tell me how to handle this. I'd lost Lana trying to help *him*.

I pushed myself off the wall and walked away as I wiped the proof of my breakdown from my face.

"Look, bro, I get it. You love her. I know that feeling real well. But crying like a fucking pussy ain't gonna do one bit of good. We have to find her. It takes big boys to do that. Think you can dry up the well and help me think this through?"

I froze and dropped my hands to my sides. What had he just said?

Turning around I stared at him. "Did you just say, 'I love her'?"

Beau rolled his eyes and crossed his arms over his chest as he leaned against the doorframe. "Really, Saw? You gotta ask me that?" He shook his head as if I were the biggest idiot on the planet. "Let me ask you something. When you lost Ash . . . did you cry? I know we beat each other up and you did a lot of yelling. But did you cry?"

"No."

Beau nodded. "Did you want to? Or were you just mad as hell?"

I thought back to those weeks after our breakup. I didn't remember fighting back tears. Not once.

"No."

"Didn't think so. 'Cause although you loved Ash, she wasn't the one. When you fall for the one who owns you, she'll be the only one that has the power to make you cry."

Chapter 20

LANA

"I'm not telling you where I am, Mom," I repeated for the fifth time.

"Lana Grace McDaniel! You are only eighteen years old. It's dangerous for you to travel alone. I am your mother! I need to know where you are. Come home. Just, wherever you are, come home. Ashton has called three times, and that Sawyer—"

"No. I don't want to hear it. I don't care. Just please, Mom, if you want to talk to me don't bring him and Ashton up, okay?"

"But they—"

"I will hang up this phone and turn it off. Do you understand me?"

I heard my mother's sharp intake of breath. I'd never spoken to her like that before, but I was tired of her. She never listened to me. She tried to control me. No longer. I was eighteen years old, but I felt so much older. I always had.

"Fine," she snapped.

"Now if there is nothing else you'd like to say, I need to go. I'll call you again soon. Trust me when I tell you I am completely safe. That's all you need to know."

"If this is about your father—"

"No, Mom, it isn't about him. Not anymore. My decisions are about me. From here on out, what I do won't take into account what you or Daddy do or say."

My mother's silence was so rare I wondered if she'd hung up on me. That would definitely be a first.

Then I heard a deep sigh. "Okay," she finally said.

"Okay," I replied.

"I love you, Lana. You know that, don't you?"

No, I didn't know it. Not really. I wasn't sure Mom understood the concept of loving someone else more than herself.

"Sure, Mom. Love you, too," I said. I'd done enough as far as honesty went for one conversation. I did love her, and I wasn't sure she could take any more of the truth.

Pressing end, I went ahead and turned off my phone before dropping it in my largest piece of luggage. Not that I thought my mom was smart enough to trace me or anything; I wasn't sure she'd even think about that method of finding me. I figured if I kept it off, unless I was checking in, then I was safe. I thought maybe I should buy one of those disposable cell phones and use it for calls from now on. I remembered an episode of CSI where that method worked.

Shaking my head at my own scheming to keep hidden from my mom, I walked over to stand in front of the large window centered in the left wall. Jewel hadn't been kidding about the view. I could see the pool to my left since we were on the bottom floor, but straight ahead was nothing except white sandy beach and the Gulf of Mexico. I could stay there the rest of the summer. Figure things out. Heal. Then go back to Alpharetta and face my future. Maybe I could get a job or two that paid well. Save up for two years and then go to the University of Georgia. Not my first choice, but it was better than staying at home and going to the community college. It would be more affordable to go to the state college than go off to Florida. Grimacing at my stupidity, I thought about all the things I'd sold on eBay once I heard the news Sawyer had signed with Florida. I'd figured if I could save up enough money, my dad would help me. I'd applied, gotten accepted, and used the small scholarship I'd received from the local ladies' club my mother was a part of to pay for my registration. I still needed so much more.

Not that it mattered. I'd have never been able to go through with it now. Maybe it was fate's way of stepping in and fixing my stupid planning. It wasn't meant for me to be at the University of Florida. I wasn't meant to be with Sawyer.

"Hey, chica, stop staring out at the gorgeous beach with that sad face and get your hot little pink bikini on and come soak up some sun with me."

I turned around to see Jewel standing in the doorway. Her long blond hair was pulled up in a high ponytail, and she was wearing a lime green string bikini that made her tan seem even darker.

"What about your date?" I asked. "And what happened to you and Heath? I thought he was spending the summer here with you." When she'd told me about her date with the life-guard, I'd been so focused on breathing through my broken heart that I hadn't processed her comment.

She waved a hand as if batting away a fly. "He caught me with this beach volleyball guy that, like, plays on a pro team. So hot, Lana, I mean *so* hot. And soooo worth it. Heath flipped his lid and left. It was for the best. We had just about squeezed all the good out of that relationship. Time to move on."

That was Jewel for you. She could jump from one guy to the next and never look back. Any guy who went into an exclusive relationship with her was just asking for trouble. Jewel couldn't do it. However, she could be a friend—maybe not the best one in the world, but she'd been the only one I'd ever really had. Right then she was a lifesaver.

"Let me get changed, and I'll meet you out there in a few minutes," I told her.

She nodded and turned to walk away. Suddenly I thought about my mom.

"Hey, Jewel," I called out.

She turned back to look at me with that carefree expression she always wore like a crown. "Yeah?"

"Don't tell my mom or dad I'm here if they call, okay?"

Jewel nodded. "No worries. I'd want to hide from those two too if they were my 'rents."

"And Ashton, if she calls . . . I don't want her to know either."

Jewel's eyes went wide in surprise. "Wow, really? What'd the ever-perfect cousin you love so much do? I can so go pull her pretty blond hair if I need to. She's a little too prissy-perfect for my taste anyway."

Shaking my head, I couldn't help but smile. Yep, Jewel might hit on the guy you like and dress slutty for confession in hopes of tempting the priest, but she'd have your back in a fight if the chance ever arose. "Ashton did nothing to me. Still love her, just need some distance from Grove right now and everyone in it."

Jewel puckered her lips as if wanting to ask more and trying to keep from doing so. She finally nodded. "Got it. Don't tell one fucking soul who inquires about you that I've seen you. Done. Now get your perky ass in a bikini and slather on some sunblock because God knows you don't need any more freckles."

Not being able to use my phone sucked. I needed something to read while I lay on the beach, and my phone had my Kindle app on it. I didn't have an actual book with me, and all Jewel had were magazines that I wasn't in the mood to read. I already knew those how-to articles did not work. I'd tried most of them.

Jewel waved happily when she glanced up at me through her hot-pink aviator sunglasses. She had a great setup out here. Two lounge chairs and a large beach umbrella, which was already tilted to shade the entire empty chair. She was bathed in the sun's rays, a magazine in her lap and a large hurricane glass in her hand.

"You look smoking, Lana Banana," she called out, then whistled.

I was beyond getting embarrassed by Jewel's comments.

I sat down in the shaded chair, leaned my head back, and sighed. This was nice. The breeze, the sound of the ocean . . .

"Here take a sip. It's got orange juice, pineapple juice, ginger ale, and vodka. It's *amazing*."

I started to shake my head but instead reached for the cup and thought, *What the hell?*

Taking a sip of the tropical flavored concoction, I realized it was really good. I could easily drink the whole thing. But I didn't. I needed some sense about me right now. Drinking away my problems was a weak thing to do.

I handed the drink back to Jewel. "Yum. Thanks."

Jewel started to stand up. "You keep it. I'll go make another."

"No, thanks. I don't want to drink. Not now anyway."

Jewel frowned and took the glass before settling back in her chair. "You gonna tell me what happened?"

No, probably not.

"Don't want to talk about it," I replied.

Jewel sighed. "Okay, fine. But be warned, I'm going to let that answer fly only for a little while. Eventually you *are* going to tell me what happened in Grove."

Fair enough. She had supplied me with an escape and she was keeping shut about it. When I was ready, she deserved an explanation.

The phone in her lap began singing "Circus" by Britney Spears. It was Jewel's theme song.

She glanced down at the phone and then up at me. "It's your mom."

I'd been prepared for this. "Answer it. Act like you haven't got a clue."

Jewel grinned. She loved the idea of getting to lie. It was ridiculous, but she liked the feeling it gave her.

"Hello?" Then she was quiet for a moment. My mom was probably talking a mile a minute. "So, wait . . . She's just missing? Have you talked to her?" Jewel winked at me. She was good at this. "Oh, wow. No, she hasn't called or anything. Should I try calling her? I can see if she answers my phone call and tells me where she's gone off to."

She was really good. Heck, I almost believed she didn't know I'd left Grove.

"Off? Ouch. Who pissed in her Wheaties?" I covered my

mouth in shock. She'd just said *pissed* while talking to my mother.

"Weird, Mrs. Mac, but no, she hasn't called me. I was hoping she would, but I haven't heard anything yet. I'll let you know if I do."

My mother hated it when Jewel called her Mrs. Mac. Actually, my mother just hated Jewel. This phone call had to be annoying her to no end.

"I gotta go, Mrs. Mac. Sorry, but my lifeguard is here and he is one yummy number, ya know? I'll call if I hear anything," she cooed, then hung up her phone. She double-checked to make sure it was disconnected before grinning up at me. "Go ahead and say it. I rocked that phone call."

If I hadn't been completely numb inside, I'd have laughed. "Yes, you were amazing. I'll never be sure if you're telling the truth again because that was completely believable. I'm almost convinced you haven't seen or heard from me."

Jewel giggled and leaned back in her chair. "Whatev, you're the only person on earth who can read through my lies. I prefer to think of it as acting. I so think I need to move to Hollywood. I'd be brilliant on the big screen. Or maybe just a CW show . . . ooooooh. I could be on *Vampire Diaries* and lure Damon away from his infatuation from Elena. Then I could do one of those naked scenes he likes to do so much."

I closed my eyes as she went on and on about a naked Damon and how amazing she'd look on television.

SAWYER

Three days and nothing. Not even her mother could find her. I was empty. Nothing mattered anymore. I didn't want to get out of bed. The only thing that kept me going was the hope that maybe one day she'd call. Maybe one day, I'd find her.

I couldn't sleep. Each night, I lay awake in my bed, staring at the ceiling and going over all the thoughtless things I'd done to her. She'd been so damn sweet too. I hadn't deserved her, but she'd wanted me. Me. No one else. Even after I called her a distraction, she'd forgiven me. When she'd needed someone to hold her and listen to her, I'd pushed her away to comfort Ashton while she threw up. She'd forgiven me for that one too. Hell, all she'd done that month was forgive me for my stupidity. I wasn't sure I could focus enough next week when I had to go to Florida for the first week of practice. How could I just leave Grove and not know Lana was okay, not get the chance to hold her and tell her how sorry I was? How could I go without being able to tell her that I was in love with her?

Picking up the nearest thing I could get my hands on, a random picture frame, I hurled it across the room and roared in frustration. Anything to release the fear, pain, and suffocating feeling of loss churning inside me.

"You put a hole in the sheetrock," Beau drawled, and I jerked my gaze toward the door to see him standing there watching me. "Your mama ain't gonna be real happy about that one, I'm guessing."

"Like I give a shit," I replied with an angry snarl.

Beau shrugged. "Just sayin' you might want to go back to pounding your fist on brick since you can't break that. Then again, you need those hands in working order for next week. Florida's gonna need their golden boy draft pick if they want any chance at taking down the Tide anytime in the next four years."

I knew he was trying to get my mind off Lana, but it was pointless. I wasn't in the mood to argue SEC football with him. At the moment, I didn't give a shit who won what. I just wanted Lana back. I dropped down to sit on the sofa behind me, and let my head fall back on the black leather.

"I gotta find her, Beau." The desperate sound in my voice wasn't lost on me.

"We will. Just takes some time. The girl doesn't want to be found. She's smart. She covered all her tracks."

She couldn't have covered everything. Someone had to have helped her. But who?

"She couldn't just disappear like that. It isn't like Grove has any damn taxis she can hail. Heck, she can't even call one because they don't exist. It's at least thirty miles to the nearest bus station. *Someone* had to have helped her. That's my missing clue."

Beau sat down on the sofa across from me. "Her mama called that friend of hers at the beach, right?"

I nodded, closing my eyes. I'd met Jewel. There was no way she just dropped everything and hauled ass that quickly to Grove to pick up Lana. No possible way. Even if she'd wanted to, she couldn't have pulled that off.

"She hadn't heard from her. Lana's mom said she was positive. She'd talked to Jewel herself, and the girl didn't have a clue. Nor was she really worried about it."

Beau frowned. "Her friend didn't care that she was missing?"

"You haven't met Jewel. She's interested in partying and guys. That's the extent of her concerns. I spent an entire meal trying to keep her hand off my dick. Trust me. The girl is shallow."

"Just because she's a party girl doesn't mean she isn't loyal to her friends. You spent what, one meal with her? I don't think that's enough time to decide about a person's loyalties. She annoyed you, but Lana doesn't seem like a girl who'd put up with someone who had no good qualities. She's pretty damn guarded. If she calls Jewel a friend, then there is something about Jewel you don't know."

Beau had a point.

"You know, you're right." I stood up and reached for my phone. I had Lana's mother's number on my speed dial.

"Who you calling?" Beau asked, leaning forward with his elbows resting on his knees.

"Lana's mom. I need Jewel's number."

Beau nodded. "Now you're thinking."

After getting Jewel's phone number and assuring Lana's mom I'd call her if I found out anything, I quickly hung up and dialed the number she'd give me.

"Hello?" a bright chipper voice said after the third ring.

"Jewel? This is Sawyer Vincent," I replied.

"Oooooooph, well, isn't this a surprise? I don't recall giving you my phone number, Sawyer Vincent. Did you miss me so much you went to the trouble of hunting it down?" she cooed into the phone. Beau was wrong about this. I was already cringing. The chick had my number and the ability to annoy the shit out of me.

"Uh, yeah, well, I'm hoping you can help me out—"

"Anything you want, I'm sure I can accommodate. I'm very talented with my hands . . . and mouth."

She didn't know how to take a hint. That much I was sure of.

"Have you spoken to Lana recently? Has she called you? I know her mom has called you and you didn't know anything, but I'm desperate. I need to find her. If there is anything you know please, please tell me. I need her. Please." I stopped begging and prayed silently this phone call wasn't in vain.

"Uh, wow. Um, what the heck happened with you two? I mean, her mom called and was worried, and I thought maybe

Lana had taken off because of her dad or something. I've been expecting her to call me, but she hasn't yet. Is this your fault? Did you hurt her?"

The small ray of hope I'd had was extinguished. I'd known better than to think Lana had run off to Jewel. Besides, it was impossible. Who would have taken her to Jewel? This girl really didn't have a clue.

"I need to speak with her. I need to see her. If she calls you or you have any idea where she could be, would you please call me? I'll pay you for your trouble; just please let me know if you can think of anything. I'm not looking for her for her mother's sake. This is for me. Just me."

"Ooooookay, Sawyer Vincent. I'll be sure to let you know if anything comes up. But dang, I'm curious now. Did little Lana Banana snag herself a guy finally? I hope so 'cause the girl is way past due."

Gripping my phone tighter, I worked on controlling the need to tell the bitch off, for the sole reason that I couldn't burn that bridge.

"Just call me if you hear anything, okay?" I repeated.

"Sure, sexy. In the meantime, you could come visit me. I'd make you real happy. I'm staying at Kiva Dunes condos on West Beach. Unit one oh three. My room is at the far corner and looks straight at the water instead of the windows facing the pool."

I tuned her out as she drawled on. The girl didn't have a

clue. "No, thanks, just, if you hear anything. Thanks." I pressed end before she could tell me how happy she could make me.

"Well?" Beau asked.

"She knows nothing. Your guess about her having some winning qualities was way off course."

"Huh" was his only reply.

Chapter 21

LANA

The music was thumping outside my window, and the strangers filling up the living area of the condo were getting louder. I would think that, since this was a condo, people in the other units would complain. But apparently this was a party hub. The speakers out at the pool were blasting dance music. I could hear the same noise going on over my head. The entire place was crazy. It wasn't a large building. It had, at the most, thirty units and, according to Jewel, they were all used by their owners. They weren't rented out. I closed my blinds to give me a little privacy. Three different people had already knocked on my door. After the second knock, I stopped answering. They were drunk guys with equally drunk girls looking for a place to have nasty, unprotected, disease-infested sex. Shuddering at the thought, I went to the private bathroom attached to my room. I was thankful for that small area of peace.

"Open this door right now, Lana!" Jewel yelled, banging on my bedroom door. Great, she was already drunk and going to force me to party.

Sighing, I headed to open the door and get it over with. I just wanted a long, hot bath.

Jerking the door open, I started to tell her I wasn't interested, but she barged past me and slammed the door behind her. She locked it, then spun around to face me.

"What the *hell* did you do to Sawyer Vincent?" she demanded, a look of awe on her face.

I didn't want to talk about Sawyer. "I told you I don't want to talk about him."

"Well, you're going to because I just lied out my ass for you while the boy begged and pleaded with me to call him if I heard from you or had any idea where you might be."

He'd called Jewel?

"When? Just now? He called you?" I asked, confused.

"*Yes*, he called me. Sexy southern drawl and all. He was pitiful I tell you. *Pi-ti-ful*. What did you do? Can you give me lessons? 'Cause girl, you must have rocked his world."

Sinking down onto the bed behind me, I stared up at her, shaking my head. Why would he be calling me? He had Ashton now. Couldn't he just be happy? Why would he be begging Jewel for help? For Ashton's sake. That was the only thing that made any sense.

"What did he say exactly?" I asked.

Jewel propped one hand on her hip and shook her head. "Oh no. You don't get to ask the questions first. I do. I ask and you answer. Then, and only then, will I tell you what was said between us."

Dang.

"Please, don't make me do this. I don't want to talk about him."

"No more begging. I've had my fill for the night, thank you very much. Now talk."

Just thinking about him made me anxious. How was I supposed to talk about him? Standing up, I began to pace in front of the bed. I could do this. I wanted to know what he said to Jewel and what she said back, because if Jewel had let anything slip, I needed to pack up and leave. I didn't want Ashton or my mom showing up here.

"I've been in love with Sawyer Vincent since I was a kid. He has been in love with Ashton for just as long. They broke up about seven months ago because she fell in love with his cousin Beau. Don't ask me why, because I can't figure it out. Sawyer is perfect. Beau is . . . well, Beau is a heathen . . . but he is insanely in love with Ashton."

"Wait, both of these boys are in love with Ashton?" Jewel asked.

"Yep. Always have been," I replied, then took a deep breath before I went on. "I thought that once Sawyer had time to get over Ashton, I would step in and make a move. Try to get his attention." The hurt, painful laugh that escaped me bordered on a sob. I hated my weakness when I mentioned his name.

"I did this whole makeover thing in hopes of attracting Sawyer. It was well past time for me to stop looking like a mouse anyway. I did it because I wanted to be a girl who could catch Sawyer's eye. And it worked. He noticed me. But it wasn't enough." Please, God, let that be enough for her. I didn't want to talk about this anymore.

"Okay, so if it wasn't enough, then why is the boy begging me to help him find you? Because from the way he sounded, you got to him a lot more than you think," Jewel assured me.

I was going to have to tell her everything, or she'd end up assuming the wrong thing and tell him where I was.

"I'm sure he did. Because when Ashton wants something, Sawyer will move mountains to get it for her."

"She's with Beau, right?" Jewel asked.

Turning from her so the tears stinging my eyes were hidden, I shook my head. "No. Beau cheated on her. I was really shocked, because he is so completely infatuated with her, but she had proof. Soon as she found out, she ran to Sawyer. He dropped me like I was on fire, and let her run straight into his arms." Sniffling, I wiped at the tears that had managed to escape. Then I looked back at Jewel.

"You mean he's desperate to find you because Ashton is upset that you left?"

All I could do was nod.

"Damn," Jewel muttered, and then an angry scowl came over her face. "I'm going to beat her pretty little face in."

"Jewel, no. Don't blame Ashton. None of this is her fault. She can't control the fact Sawyer loves her. They were a couple for three years. He's her safe place."

"This sucks balls. You know that, right?" The disgust on her face almost made me smile. Almost.

"Yes, it does. But I walked into this. I took a chance." Shrugging, I walked over to sit back down beside her on the bed. "We both know it was time I started taking chances. I crashed and burned, but I learned from it."

Jewel wrapped her arm around my shoulders and pulled my head against her. "Ah, damn. This sucks." She sighed. "I won't tell him anything. He did beg and plead with me to call him if I heard from you or I thought of somewhere you could be. He said he 'needed' to find you. I was mistaken with his anxious tone. I figured you'd wrapped the boy around your finger and gotten angry with him and left him high and dry. I didn't realize he was trying to ease some other girl's guilt. She may be your cousin, but I am not a fan. Just sayin'."

We sat in silence for a while. Finally I sat back up. "Thank you for lying. I have complete faith in your acting abilities."

Jewel smirked. "So you wanna run off to LA with me? We could rock that town. You and I."

A real laugh managed to bubble up, and I shook my head. "Not right now. Maybe someday soon."

"Come out here and party. Forget everything. Drink one of my tropical drinks. I have one I make with coconut rum that is to die for."

I wasn't ready. "Give me a few more days?"

"Sure, babe."

SAWYER

Sawyer was always the Vincent boy worth fighting for. He's the special one.

I reread that last line for what felt like the hundredth time. I was packed up and headed to Florida. It had been over a week, and no Lana. No sign of her. No text. Her phone still went directly to voice mail. She'd called her mother again to check in, but the number had been unknown and her mother hadn't been able to trace it. All I knew is she was alive. That small amount of knowledge kept me from losing my mind. I lived for those calls from her mom telling me what Lana had said. It was my only connection to her, and, although I wasn't a fan of her parents, I was starting to have an odd sort of affection for her crazy mother. She did love Lana even if she sucked at showing her. The woman was definitely controlling, but Lana was doing a number on her then and I was willing to bet that relationship would be forever changed for the better.

Folding the note Lana had left Ash into the worn creases where I'd opened and read it and then folded it again, I slipped it into my pocket. I didn't go anywhere without it. Having it close to me reminded me that when I found her, I could fix this. She'd misunderstood, and it was my fault. If I'd have opened my eyes and realized I was in love with the girl, that wouldn't have happened. Unfortunately, Lana hadn't known. She thought I still loved Ash.

"Sawyer, you ready?" my dad called from the foyer. I wasn't ready. I didn't want to leave Grove. What if she came back and I was gone? Besides, how the hell was I supposed to concentrate enough to throw a football? The week was going to be a disaster.

"Coming, Dad," I called back. I grabbed my phone so I could look again at the picture Ash had texted me from our trip to the mountains. Lana had been hiking up the rocks toward the waterfall in Cheaha, and Ash had snapped a picture of her just as she'd glanced back laughing. It was the only picture I had of her. I'd had it printed and framed so I could keep it by my bed. Some nights staring at it was the only thing that kept me going. I slipped my phone into my pocket. I had my note and my picture. It would have to get me through the next few days.

When I got to the bottom of the steps, Ethan was standing in the foyer talking to my dad. His eyes met mine and something felt off. There was something I was missing.

"Ethan?"

He shuffled his feet. "Hey, Sawyer I, uh, forgot you were heading out today."

I hadn't been to a field party, or anywhere else for that matter, since Lana left me. "Yeah, practice is starting up."

"I came by to ask you something, but it can wait until you get back."

"You're here now, might as well ask."

God help him if he asked me if Lana was available. I'd break his damn neck.

"Uh, it's about Lana . . . ," he began.

I looked over at my dad. "Can you give us a sec, Dad?"

Frowning, my father nodded, grabbed one of my bags, and headed outside.

"What about Lana?" I asked, making sure he heard the warning in my words.

Ethan sighed. "Not sure how to ask this . . . ," he began.

"I'd choose my words carefully, bro," I replied.

He nodded. "Yeah, I'm getting that loud and clear." Clearing his throat, he shifted his feet again. "Do you, uh, love her? Lana, that is."

The fact he'd felt the need to clarify it was Lana he was asking about pissed me off. I didn't like her being compared to Ashton. She was so much more than what I'd had with Ashton. There was no comparison.

"Yes," I said in a clipped tone.

"I mean, do you love her more than—"

"Don't you *fucking* say it," I said with a snarl. That was a cliff Ethan didn't want to step off. His eyes widened in surprise.

"Okay. I get it." He backed away and moved toward the door.

"That's all you wanted to say? Find out if Lana was available? You know she left me, right? No one can find her."

Ethan swallowed hard and shook his head slowly. "Uh, no, I mean I heard something. I wasn't sure."

"I gotta go if that's all you needed."

Ethan turned and headed out the front door. "Good luck in Florida. I'll, uh, see ya when you get back. Looking forward to hearing about it. The rest of us are going to have to live vicariously through you and Beau now. Since our football days are over."

His voice was still tense, but I could tell he was trying to calm me down. If I were a good friend, I'd apologize. Right then I couldn't. I'd do it the next time I saw him. Slipping my hand in my pocket, I rubbed Lana's letter gently between my fingers. I had to find her.

Chapter 22

LANA

My freckles were just getting worse. SPF eighty wasn't even helping. Sure, my skin wasn't red, but my freckles were getting a tan. Not something I wanted. Even so, this was good therapy. Lying out here in my safe, shaded area made me feel like I was hidden from the world. I was hidden from everyone who had the power to hurt me. Too bad it was a fleeting thing. I'd have to leave at the end of the month and head back to Alpharetta and my mother. I did not want to think about that. Facing her, after hiding away for over a month, would be difficult. But I was still checking in.

She kept trying to get me to talk about Sawyer. It always ended with me hanging up. I figured she'd eventually stop it. Maybe when we got the wedding invitation from Ashton in a few years, she'd finally let go of her hopes that Sawyer Vincent was interested in me. My stomach rolled, and I fought off the sick feeling that thought instigated.

"Lana?" A familiar voice interrupted my thoughts, and I shifted around to see Ethan standing behind the chair in which Jewel normally lounged. She wasn't there that day. She'd taken off on a shoe-buying splurge.

"Ethan?" I replied in shock. I hadn't expected to see him again.

"Hey, uh, sorry to just show up, but you can't exactly be reached by phone these days."

Oh. He'd tried to call. That surprised me. "It's okay. Do you want to sit down?"

He looked down at the chair beside me and thought about it a minute before he walked around and took a seat. He must have intended to stay awhile.

"So what's this about? Is there something you wanted to tell me?"

Ethan didn't lie back in the chair. He sat on the edge facing me, his elbows resting on his knees. His head was under the shade of the umbrella, and the serious expression on his face worried me. If this was about Sawyer, I wasn't ready for that.

"You, uh, enjoying yourself?" he asked.

"Yes, but I have a feeling you didn't just drive an hour and a half to ask me if I was enjoying myself."

Ethan chuckled and shook his head. "No, I didn't."

"Didn't think so. Spill it, Ethan."

"It's about Sawyer—"

"Never mind. Shut it, Ethan. I retract that. I don't want to know what you have to say." I reached for my bag and started to stand up. "If you want to visit and talk about the weather and try one of Jewel's tropical drinks, you are more than welcome. But I will not talk about Sawyer."

"Wait. Please don't go," he begged, standing up with me.

"Are you going to ignore my wishes?" I asked.

His shoulders slumped and he shook his head. "No. I won't bring him up."

Sitting back down, I put my bag beside me and reached inside to get a granola bar. I grabbed an extra one and handed it to Ethan, who had also sat down again.

"Here, have a granola bar."

He reached for it and gave me a weak smile. "Thanks."

We sat in silence and ate our granola bars. Once I finished mine, I turned to look at him. His face was troubled, and I almost asked him if Sawyer was okay. The fear that Sawyer could be hurt or sick battled with the fear Ethan would tell me something I couldn't handle.

"So when do you leave for college?" I asked, trying to think of anything other than Sawyer.

"Next month and you?"

I hated admitting this to anyone. Nevertheless, it was time I faced the facts. "Not sure. I've had a change of plans due to my dad's sudden lack of money. So I'll be going to the local community college the next two years. I've got to figure out what to do after, but I have time. Plenty of it." The sourness from speaking the words aloud settled in my mouth.

"Wow, I'm sorry, Lana. I always imagined you going to an Ivy League or something."

"Nope, not me." I'd been worried about things other than my education. Bad move.

"Have you talked to Ash?" he asked.

"Don't want to talk about her either if you don't mind. And the answer is no."

He was determined to discuss Sawyer with me. Did he want to know if it was clear for him to ask me out? Surely, he didn't want to give that train wreck another try. I'd been a horrible date.

"Beau didn't cheat," he blurted out quickly.

Why did that news hurt? Why the heck did I care that Sawyer had been dissed for Beau yet again? If Beau hadn't cheated, then Ash was still with him. She was crazy in love with the guy. Why, why, *why?* I shouldn't have cared that Sawyer was alone. I shouldn't have cared that he got what was coming to him. I shouldn't have.

It does not matter. If not this time, there will be a next and a next and a next, and each time, Sawyer will go running back to her—hoping, waiting, and breaking his heart and mine in the process.

"Let's not talk about Beau, either, okay. Actually, let's not talk about anyone in Grove, except you," I replied with a stern tone that I felt guilty for using. Ethan was nothing but nice.

"Just thought you'd like to know," he replied, shifting in his seat.

"Don't care. I closed that door. Or rather it was slammed in my face and I walked away after adding a padlock."

"You know, sometimes things aren't what they seem—" he began, and I held up my hand to stop him.

"Stop. I don't know why you're here. But if it's because Sawyer or Asthon put you up to it, I'm asking you as a friend to please leave."

Ethan let out a weary sigh. "No one knows where you are. I kept your secret. Like I promised. I just thought maybe I could come explain some things for them."

"Why? Why would you explain anything for them? If I'm not mistaken, you were interested in me, and Sawyer came and swooped in and took me right out of your grasp. Am I wrong about that?"

Ethan let out a hard laugh and shook his head. "No, you got it right."

"Okay, then why are you here trying to help Sawyer smooth things over?"

"Because he's my friend," Ethan replied. "And so are you."

He was such a nice guy. Bless his heart; he had no idea what he was mixed up in. This was not fixable.

"Well, then, you need better friends," I muttered.

"Sawyer had never poached on any girl he thought his friends might be interested in. When he acted the way he did with you, I didn't like it, but I knew something was different. You must've gotten to him in a way no one else did because he was not acting like himself."

"I was a means to get back at Ashton," I replied sourly.

"Maybe in the beginning you were, Lana. I thought that too at one point. I *know* now that it changed. It became something more."

"Not enough. Whatever it became, it wasn't enough. No one will be able to compete with her." The tears blurring my eyes just pissed me off. I was not going to cry again.

"There's no competition," he said softly, and I refused to cry in front of him.

"Just go, Ethan. Please." I turned my head away from him and closed my eyes. After a minute of silence, I heard him stand up and walk away.

Silent tears streamed down my face as the words "There's no competition" replayed over and over again in my head.

*   *   *

SAWYER

I hadn't been home an hour when Beau called me. He asked me to meet him down at the bar for a game of pool. I'd tried to tell him I just wanted to take a hot shower, two Tylenol, and get in bed. My body ached. How the heck did he not want to curl up and crash too? Besides, what about Ashton? Didn't he want to go see her?

Pulling into the gravel parking lot, I looked around for Beau's truck. I found it over by the far end of the building. Ethan's Jeep was right beside it. I needed to apologize to him anyway. I stepped out of my truck and headed for the door.

It was a slow night, but then not many people came to the bar on a Wednesday. Thursday through Sunday was the busy time there. I'd been only a few times with Beau, but I'd passed the place several times. I knew which nights had a full parking lot.

"Well, if it ain't my favorite nephew," Aunt Honey called out from behind the bar.

I nodded my head in her direction. "Hey, Aunt Honey."

"Want a beer? I can already tell you that you're probably gonna need it."

What the heck did that mean? I started to tell her no and then figured if I couldn't have a hot shower and painkillers, a beer, was the next best thing. "Sure, thanks."

"Go on over to the boys. They're waiting on ya. I'll bring ya a beer in just a sec."

"Yes, ma'am," I replied.

"Told ya not to call me ma'am. Makes me sound like somebody's mama," she teased, and shot me a wink.

She really was a piece of work.

I made my way over to Beau, who was leaning up against the edge of a pool table with his ankles crossed and a frosty mug of beer in his hand. It was the expression on his face that tipped me off that this wasn't just a friendly gathering. I was here for a purpose. Slipping my hand into my pocket, I held Lana's letter between my fingers. Remembering her words helped me deal. If this was bad news, I needed a reminder that she was out there and that she loved me.

"What is it, Beau?" I demanded the moment I was close enough.

"I got some answers for you that you're gonna want. But you need to remain calm while you get those answers."

My heart sped up and I froze. "Lana?"

Beau nodded. "Yep. Lana."

"You know where she is?"

"Yeah, I do. But it ain't my story to tell." Beau turned his head and I followed his gaze to Ethan, who standing a few feet away from us. "Go ahead, E., before he loses it."

Ethan shifted his gaze from me to Beau, and I could see the fear in his eyes.

"What do you know?" I started toward him, ready to

shake him until he told me what he knew.

Beau's hand clamped down on my shoulder and stopped me. "You won't get your answers if you hurt him." He turned to Ethan. "Ethan, tell him. I told you, I won't let him rip your balls off."

My heart started racing, and the blood boiled in my veins. The idea that Ethan had somehow had a hand in Lana's disappearance was making it hard for me to take calm, steady breaths.

"You better do this quick, E., 'cause he's gonna blow in a second, and I'm sore as shit from this week. I really don't want to have to stop this," Beau said, urging.

"Okay, yeah. Um, well, you see, Sawyer. I got a call from Lana—"

"Why the hell is she calling you?" I demanded, taking another step toward Ethan, who backed up a step.

"Get the fuck on with this, E.," Beau said with a growl as his hand tightened on my shoulder.

"No. Before. She called me before. The day Ash thought Beau cheated. She called me that day and told me she needed a favor. She said she couldn't stay here anymore and needed my help. I picked her up and—"

"*Where is she?*" I roared, taking another step his way. Both of Beau's hands clamped down on my shoulders.

"Easy, bro," he warned.

"Lord have mercy, boy. Drink this beer and chill out. The girl is safe, and if you'll let the kid talk, you'll find out where she's at." Aunt Honey stood in front of me and shoved a mug of beer into my hand. "Here, hold this. That way you can hit him with only one fist."

"Go on, Mama. I got this," Beau said behind me.

"Hmph, don't look like it. But I hope you're right. I ain't payin' for no repairs if he goes bat-shit in here," she replied.

Setting the beer down on the edge of the pool table, I didn't take my eyes off Ethan. He knew where she was. He *knew* where she was.

"I took her to her friend's condo at the beach."

She wasn't there. I'd called Jewel. . . . Wait. He'd taken her there?

"Did you see Jewel? Did she actually go into a condo?" I asked, hoping that I'd been played by that crazy ass friend of hers.

"Yeah, I carried her bags to the door. Jewel came outside squealing and all happy to see her. Then I went back . . . ," Ethan began.

The words that he went back sent off a possessive blaze of fury. I shrugged off Beau's grasp and stalked over to tower above Ethan. "What does that *mean*? *You went back*?"

"Not so fast. He ain't finished. Don't fuck him up now," Beau said with a growl, hooking his arms in both of mine from behind and pulling me back.

Ethan wiped at his forehead nervously and gulped. "Listen, man, I didn't know. I thought you'd moved on. I didn't know how you felt about Lana. When I came to your house Saturday to talk to you about Lana, that was the first time I realized that I'd made a huge mistake helping her run away. So I went back. I was going to fix it. She wouldn't listen to me. Hell, I couldn't even say your name."

"She was there? When did you go?" I was backing up. I needed to know. I had to get to her.

"She's there. At the condo. Condo unit one oh three. Kiva Dunes," he called out, and I started running for the door.

Then the words from the phone conversation with Jewel came back to me: *In the meantime, you could come visit me. I'd make you real happy. I'm staying at Kiva Dunes condos on West Beach. Unit one oh three. My room is on the far corner looking straight at the water instead of the windows facing the pool.* The crazy bitch wasn't so crazy after all. I'd bet my ass the room was Lana's. Jewel was trying to tell me without ratting out Lana. Beau was right. Lana was careful with who she let get close. Jewel was one helluva liar, though. I'd completely believed her. The dumb blonde thing she had going really threw me off.

I reached for my truck door and realized my hands were shaking. I knew where Lana was. And I was going to get her back.

Chapter 23

LANA

I couldn't stay in this room one more night. Of course, I didn't want to go out into that wild mess, either. Before it got too carried away, I locked the door to my room and went to the window to escape. I didn't want anyone making themselves at home in my bed while I was out. I didn't think any of them would attempt to get in the window. I'd been locked away for two weeks. Everyone knew, by now, that my room was off-limits.

Making sure no one saw my escape, I headed down to the water. Just a long walk to stretch my legs and breathe in the clean ocean air, and then I'd head back to hole up for the night. Maybe I wouldn't be so restless. Breaking into a jog, I pushed all those memories that tended to creep in when I let my guard down to the back of mind. I imagined myself running from all of them, leaving them in the past as my hair flew out behind me. Silent tears streamed down my face as I let it go . . . one memory at a time.

SAWYER

This place was like a frat house. I didn't like that. I didn't like it at all. I started to knock on the door as music began to pound through the thin walls. Some bikini-clad girls leaned over the railing on the second floor and called out what they wanted to do to me if I'd just come on up. Shaking my head, I headed for the corner room that faced the ocean.

A guy had a girl pressed up against the side of the building, and I was more than positive they were having sex. This crap had surrounded Lana for two weeks. I was going to kill Ethan once I got back home. She didn't belong here. If someone had touched her . . . I stopped myself. I couldn't do this. I had to win her back. If I went all caveman, she would fight me.

Turning the corner, the window facing the ocean greeted me. I glanced at the other windows in the unit, and they all faced the pool. The window had to belong to Lana's room. I knocked and waited, but there was nothing but silence. The lights were off. Could she actually be somewhere in this wild bunch of people? I reached down and thought I'd check and see if the window was locked. It wasn't. Not smart, Lana. Didn't she know better than to leave her windows unlocked? Anyone could have gotten in. I didn't want to think about it. I needed to focus.

Pushing the window open, I stepped inside the room. The sweet smell of her perfume filled the room. Jewel had given me directions straight to Lana, and I'd missed the cue. The room was empty. I glanced over toward the door and realized it was locked. So she'd escaped through the window. She wasn't at this party.

She'd be back. I just needed to wait. I was close.

Sitting down on the bed, I reached over and took a pillow. Holding it to my nose, I inhaled. God, I'd missed that smell. Burying my face in her scent, I sat watching the window . . . waiting.

LANA

The tears were dried on my face as I made my way back to the condo. I'd run for over an hour. My lungs burned and my legs would probably feel like Jell-O tomorrow. I wasn't big on exercise, so it was gonna hurt.

Pulling up my window, I stepped inside to find someone sitting on my bed in the dark. Naturally, I screamed.

"Lana, it's me." Sawyer's hands were on my arms instantly. Sawyer . . . Sawyer was here.

I stood, frozen, trying to decide if I'd passed out from the running and it was a dream.

"I didn't mean to scare you. I'm sorry." The words "I'm sorry" snapped me out of my shocked haze, and I jerked out of his grasp and quickly moved away from him and toward the door.

"Lana, please don't. Please listen to me. Don't shut me out. You have no idea—"

"I have no idea? *Me?* Yes, I have an idea. I want you to leave. Do you understand me? *Leave.* I. Do. Not. Want. To. See. You!" I was yelling, but I knew no one would hear me over the noise outside.

"Lana, please," Sawyer begged. He walked hesitantly toward me. I closed my eyes and crossed my arms protectively over my chest. I hated how the pleading sound in his voice pulled at me.

"If you *ever* felt one small amount of anything for me, you'll leave and let me move on," I whispered fiercely.

When he didn't respond, I was torn between joy that he was leaving, meaning he felt something for me, no matter how small it may be, relief that he wouldn't be here to witness me crumble to the floor, and agony, because seeing him had completely ripped me open.

I heard the faint rattle of paper, and I opened my eyes slowly to see Sawyer standing in the same spot, a worn-looking letter in his hands. He began to read:

"I made the mistake of opening my heart up to someone who clearly could never feel the same about me. I knew Sawyer loved you. I've known it since we were kids. I thought maybe just getting his attention for a short time would be enough. It wasn't."

My chest felt like it was going to explode. He had the letter I'd left Ashton. Oh, God.

He lifted his eyes from the paper and looked directly at me with so much pain, and something else, in his eyes. . . . "I loved Ashton once. She was my childhood crush. She was all I really knew. But when she left me, I didn't cry. When you left me, I wept like a baby."

I stopped breathing as he lowered his eyes back to the paper in his hands.

"I've grown up with two parents who never once thought about me in the choices they made. My emotions weren't something they concerned themselves with, and maybe that is my fault because I didn't speak up. I just pushed the hurt and anger deep inside me. I wanted to be strong because I knew they were weak. I'm tired of being strong. I'm tired of being second best. I need someone to love me."

He stopped reading and lifted his eyes to stare at me once again. "You should never and I mean, *never*, be anyone's second choice. Anyone who doesn't see you for the incredible gift you are is a blind bastard."

He lowered his eyes back to the paper and began reading again.

"Staying in Grove isn't a possible option for me. I let myself hope for too much. I've been broken too many times. I can't stay somewhere near . . . someone who will eventually destroy me." His green eyes lifted to meet mine, and the tears glistening in them took my breath away. "If I lose you because of the blind idiot I've been, then I will be the one who is destroyed."

He continued to read.

"You had the right Vincent boy all along. Don't take him for granted this time. He loves you in a way that I hope to one day inspire in someone. He would give up the world for you. When you have someone that special, that incredible who loves you, don't let it go. This is your second chance to treasure what you've had all your life. Sawyer was always the Vincent boy worth fighting for. He's the special one."

Sawyer slowly folded the paper and rubbed his thumb over it as if it were something precious. Then tucked it back into his pocket.

"Ashton didn't have the right Vincent boy. I know this because I understand now what love really feels like. The kind that consumes you. Love holds the power to break you, holds the power to complete you. When I read this letter, I was standing in Ashton's living room after fixing things for her and Beau, which was all I wanted to do. They belong together. They've always belonged together. I get that now. Not because she chose him, but because you chose me. Until you, I was lost. I thought Ashton was what my life was supposed to be. Letting go of the comfort zone that our relationship represented was hard. Then you came into my life like a light bursting through the darkness. You made everything make sense." He took a step closer to me, and I fought the urge to throw myself in his arms. "Lana. I think about you every minute of every day. When I'm with you, my world is complete. When I touch you, I understand the meaning of life. When I lost you, I completely shattered. You. Own. Me."

A tear rolled down my face and dropped from my chin. That wasn't enough.

This time I needed more.

Sawyer reached out for my hand and pulled me closer to him.

I wanted to melt in his arms, but I couldn't.

"I love you, Lana. I love you so much. Everything about you. The way your lips curl up slowly when you smile, the freckle right under your perfect little bottom, the way your laughter sends warmth flooding through my veins, how your touch lights me on fire. I love you, and I will spend the rest of my life making sure you know that you are my number one. You will always be my number one."

That was it. That was enough. That was all I'd ever need to hear.

Chapter 24

LANA

"Crazy Girl" by the Eli Young Band woke me up from a very good dream. Stretching, I felt Sawyer's arms tighten around me. "Crazy girl, don't you know that I love you?" kept playing, and I turned to look up at Sawyer, who was reaching for my phone.

"Why is my phone turned on, and why is it singing a country song?" I asked groggily as he looked at the screen and then dropped his gaze to mine.

"It's your mom. Talk to her or she'll worry."

I gaped at him. "My mom? But—"

"I got your phone out of your bag last night and turned it on. Finding you had my adrenaline pumping, so calming down was hard to do. I changed your ringtone to the song that makes me think about you." He lowered his mouth to mine and sang, "Have

I told you lately, I love you like crazy, girl?" along with my ringing phone. I couldn't get mad at him while he was doing something like that. Early-morning, singing-Sawyer was just too freaking sweet. Even if he'd made it possible for my mom to call me.

Sighing, I took the phone from him and answered. "Hi, Mom."

"Oh, Lana, you've turned your phone back on. I'm so glad. Does this mean you're going to come home? I'm so ready to see you."

"No, I'm not coming home. Not yet, anyway." I met Sawyer's gaze and wondered what I was going to do. I wasn't sure I'd be welcomed back at Aunt Sarah's after I'd run off like that. "I don't really know what I'm going to do next."

"Why are you doing this? Is it still about Sawyer? I can tell you that—"

"Mom, it isn't about Sawyer," I replied, reaching up and running my hand through his messy hair. "He's perfect. I just don't really know yet how I'm going to finish my summer."

Sawyer frowned, and his arms tightened around me like I was going to vanish into thin air.

"Wait, did you just say Sawyer was perfect? I thought you were mad at him. I mean, I agree with you he is a lovely young man. We've spoken a lot over the past two weeks, and I think he really loves you. The boy has been so upset. He calls me all the time to see if I've heard from you, even though every time you called, I called him right away and told him what you said and that you were fine. Oh, no. I didn't mean to tell you that. Don't be mad at me, honey. He was just so worried."

I smirked at him. "He can be pretty persuasive. I understand."

"He's a very good catch, Lana. Wealthy family and going to Florida for college too. I was so surprised when he told me he had gotten a scholarship there for football. That's perfect."

"No, Mom, it isn't. Dad isn't going to be able to help out." Saying that never got easier.

"Nonsense. Yes, he is going to help. The alimony he gives me every month will more than pay for it. Besides, I'm selling the house and downsizing. It's too much house for just me."

"Mom, no, you love the house, and I don't think you understand how much it'll cost with books and living expenses—"

"I'm not an idiot, Lana. I checked into all of that while you've been gone. You're still getting mail, and I had to pay a few more fees and get the first semester paid for. I've held off buying things for your dorm room until you come home to help me."

"Lana, what's wrong?" Sawyer sat up quickly and pulled me up in his arms.

"Is that Sawyer? Are you back in Grove?" my mother asked, and I patted Sawyer's chest to silently calm him down. I'd become teary-eyed listening to my mother, and he'd gone into panic mode.

"Yes, that's Sawyer. He, uh, found me last night," I replied into the phone while smiling at Sawyer, who was watching me carefully with frown lines between his eyebrows.

"Found you? Where are you? How did he find you?"

"I've been with Jewel all along. She covered for me, and honestly, I have no idea how he found me, unless . . ." I paused before I finished that thought. I didn't want to have to explain this all to my mother, and she would want to know. I was pretty sure who'd ratted me out. Ethan was the only one in Grove who knew where I had gone.

"Listen, Mom, I'll call you later. I've got to figure some things out today, but I'll be sure to let you know. Let me talk to Sawyer, okay, and thank you. I love you."

"I love you, too, Lana."

I disconnected and laid my phone down beside me before crawling on top of Sawyer. "So how'd you get my whereabouts out of Ethan? And is he still alive?"

Sawyer chuckled and shifted me so I was straddling him. "Yes, he's still breathing. Actually, I left him completely unharmed. I ran out of there so fast once I had your location, I didn't even say good-bye."

"Good, now tell me how you got it out of him," I replied, running my hands up his bare chest. I'd missed touching him.

"He just told me," he said in a husky whisper. His attention was focused on my hands as I traced circles around his very firm pecs.

"The guilt got to him, I guess," I murmured before leaning down to press a kiss to the bruise just over his ribs. "Did those big mean football players hurt you?" I cooed, raining a trail of kisses across his abs and back up his chest.

"Uh-huh, I can show you a lot of other places they hurt me too." He sighed, running his hands down my back to cup my butt.

"Mmkay, just let me finish kissing these booboos, and I'll get to the other ones next," I promised.

"Please, take your time," he said with a groan, slipping his hands inside my panties.

"You still haven't answered me about how you got my hide-out location from Ethan," I reminded him as I slid down his body so I could kiss just below his belly button.

"Gaaah, baby." He arched into me then took a ragged breath. "Who's Ethan?" he asked in a low deep voice.

I lifted my eyes to meet his fascinated gaze. "You remember Ethan. Your friend who told on me," I reminded before I licked gently at the skin right above his boxers.

"Oh, fuuuuuck," he moaned, tangling his hands in my hair.

I decided to let the Ethan thing go. I was having too much fun watching the guy I loved come apart in my arms. Slipping a finger under the top of his boxers, I leaned forward and whispered in his ear. "Any booboos down there I need to pay attention to?"

"Oh yeah, lots and lots," he croaked out.

SAWYER

"Dad," I called out in way of a greeting as I knocked once on his office door and stepped inside. He was sitting behind the large mahogany desk that he'd had shipped over from somewhere he and Mom had visited. I didn't remember the details.

"Sawyer," he replied, looking up from the paperwork on his desk. "How was practice?"

"Good. I'm going to learn a lot this year. Being red-shirted was a smart move."

Dad nodded in agreement.

"Beau had a good week too. They're starting him on the offensive line." It drove me nuts that he never asked about his other son. The one he ignored. The one he never claimed.

Dad frowned and looked back down at his paperwork. "That's good. Your cousin has always excelled as a receiver."

"You mean my brother. Beau's not my cousin. He's my brother." I'd never forced my dad to face this. I'd been so angry with Beau about Ashton when this all came out, I'd let this slide. If Beau didn't want to deal with it then I'd figured why should I? But it wasn't fair. This farce my dad lived wasn't fair.

Clearing his throat, he took off his reading glasses and leaned back in his chair to level his gaze on me. "You want to talk about that? Is that what this is about?"

"Yeah, it is. I want to talk about that." I didn't snap. I kept my tone level. Yelling wouldn't get me anywhere.

"Beau is biologically mine, yes. But I didn't raise him. I didn't love his mother. Your uncle did. Not me. I do not see Beau as my son. My nephew, yes."

"But he is your *son*. His dad died when he was six years old. He's needed a *dad* for twelve years now, and you've done nothing. Not once did you check on him. Not once did you tell him you were proud of him. Not once did you make his life easier." I stopped as my voice got louder and louder.

"Tell him I was proud of him? For what? Being a loser? Coming to football practice with a hangover? Spending time in bars? What the hell was I supposed to be proud of? Huh? Please tell me that."

My hands balled into fists, and I took a deep breath. I was so close to taking a swing at my own dad. "He was stuck with Aunt Honey, who left him at home alone when he was just a kid. If he hadn't lived in a trailer park where people deal drugs and God knows what else, maybe he would've known better. But he didn't. He made mistakes. He had to learn things the hard way. He had to learn everything the hard way. Because *you weren't there*." I pointed my finger at my dad and snarled. "Beau straightened himself out. He got a football scholarship to the *University of Alabama* for crying out loud. He found a way to make money so he could buy himself a truck. He loves his mama and takes care of her even though she did nothing to earn his help. Why? Because he loves her. She's all he has ever had. He made himself, and what he made is one damn fine man. I am so proud to call him my brother I am bursting with it when I see him. And *you*, you did nothing. Not one damn thing to make him. Nothing," I finished, and turned to leave his office. I didn't want to stay here. Not under this roof. Not with him.

"You're right," my dad's voice called out after me, and I stopped and squeezed my eyes closed tightly before turning back around to look at him.

"I wasn't there. I let him figure it all out on his own. I was afraid of your mother finding out. I was afraid of this town finding out. I didn't want to lose this life I'd built for myself. You're wrong about one thing, though. I did check on him. Why do you think you got away with sneaking out to go get him out of jams or going to stay with him when he was alone? Did you think you were just that good at being sneaky? You weren't. When you left to go to him, I followed you. I watched you both. I watched as you fixed his problems, got him out of messes, and stayed by his side when he was alone. I was always there. I was proud of you for being there for him when I wasn't. I'm not proud of myself, Sawyer. I'll live with this regret the rest of my life. Nevertheless, I am proud of Beau. He has turned into the man I always hoped he would be. He's tougher than you because of the life he lived. He is harder around the edges, but he's a good boy." My dad reached down and opened the drawer in his desk that he had always kept locked. He pulled out a large scrapbook and laid it on the desk. "Go ahead, take a look."

I walked over and opened the leather binding to see pictures of Beau as a baby. Pictures of the two of us in our football helmets when they were bigger than we were. Each page held memories of Beau's life. Every article where he'd been mentioned in the paper had been carefully clipped and placed in the pages. After I turned the last page, I saw a picture of Beau in his practice gear, standing on the field at Bryant–Denny stadium last week during practice. Lifting my eyes, I stared at my father and saw a man I didn't know existed.

"I went to both your practices last week. You both made me proud."

Shaking my head, trying to take this all in, I sank down into the chair behind me. "Why don't you reach out to him? If you have all this, you have to love him. You have to care about him. Why aren't you doing something about it? He needs you, too."

"He hates me and I don't blame him," Dad said, taking the binder and placing it back in the drawer.

"Hell yeah, he hates you. You're his father, and he thinks you care nothing for him."

"You know Beau. Better than anyone. Do you really think he'd listen to me? That he'd forgive me?"

"Dad, he doesn't have to forgive you. He doesn't have to like you. But he needs to know you love him. That you're proud of him. All you have to do is tell him. How he handles it or takes it isn't what's important. What's important is that he knows. What's important is that you tell him."

Dad sat down at his desk and neither of us spoke. There was nothing more to say.

Chapter 25

LANA

My mother was sitting on Aunt Sarah's couch, drinking tea, when Sawyer and I stepped into the living room.

"Mom?" My aunt and uncle had welcomed me back and assured me they were just glad I was safe. They didn't know the details but understood I had a lot going on with my parents.

"Lana." My mother smiled at me and then turned her smile to Sawyer. "Hello, Sawyer."

"Hello, Ms. McDaniel," he replied politely.

"I didn't know you were coming for a visit," I said, trying to figure out what was going on.

"Paperwork came that you needed to sign, and I figured we could go do that shopping for your dorm room," she explained.

I hadn't told Sawyer about Florida yet. I was afraid my

mother was being optimistic, and we might not actually be able to make it work. "Oh, um, okay . . ." I trailed off, trying to think of a way to get Sawyer out of here before Mom said anything else about college.

"Would it be okay if I came too? Lana did get to help pick out my dorm necessities, so it's only fair I get to help pick hers out," Sawyer drawled in an amused voice as he walked over to sit down in my uncle's recliner.

"Of course. That would be lovely! Wouldn't that be lovely, Lana?" my mother asked a little too enthusiastically.

How was I going to get out of this one?

"Mom, we need to make sure everything is squared away and okay before we go buying dorm stuff. I mean, there is still a chance this might not work and I'll need to stay home two years and go to a community college. What if the house doesn't sell?"

Sawyer sat up from his relaxed position and leaned forward. "What? Why might this not work? I was under the impression it was a done deal." He was directing his question to my mother like he knew what the heck he was talking about.

"Sawyer—" I began, and was cut off by my mom.

"It is Sawyer," she said soothingly. "Lana, the house is sold. I made enough money to pay for all four years of your education and buy myself a nice-size condo on the beach. That way, when you run off and leave me for Florida, I can still be close enough to my sister when I need some company."

She said Florida. Would Sawyer think I was chasing him? Smothering him? Cringing, I forced myself to meet his gaze. He grinned, stood up, and walked over to me.

Both of his hands wrapped around my waist, and he pulled me up against him and bent his head down to whisper in my ear, "Did you really think I would be this excited about college if I thought I'd be leaving my girl behind?"

"You knew." I breathed a sigh of relief.

"Yes, I knew. And if you for one second try and back out of following me to Florida, I will personally kidnap you and haul you there with me," he teased and then pressed a trail of kisses across my face until his mouth hovered over mine. "I'm not losing you again. You're with me. I want you there beside me. Always."

BEAU

Sawyer bailed on me this morning—for a girl. I couldn't help but smile. I was the one who normally bailed on workouts. It was a nice change for it to be him not showing up. I couldn't imagine why he'd want to go shopping with Lana and her *mom*. That woman was whack. Not to mention it was shopping. Who goes shopping with their girl? Then again, Ash had never asked me to go shopping with her. If she asked, I'd go.

Running down the bleachers, I slowed my pace. This had been my hundredth trip up and down. It was time for weights.

When I reached the bottom, I wiped my forehead with my towel and took a long swig from the water bottle I'd left on the bottom bleacher.

"Hello, Beau." The deep familiar voice behind me wasn't one I cared for. Putting my water down, I slung my towel over my shoulder and turned around to face Harris Vincent, my "uncle," my biological father.

"Sawyer isn't here," I replied, and headed down the last few steps and toward the field house.

"I'm not here to see Sawyer. I'm here to see you," Harris called out, and I stopped walking. Me? He wanted to talk to me? His dirty little secret? I turned back around.

"What?" was the only response he was getting out of me. I would stand there and listen to what he had to say for one reason and one reason only—Sawyer.

"I, uh, I saw your practice last week. You looked good out there."

My practice? What the hell was he talking about? I had practices in Tuscaloosa. Surely, he didn't mean those.

"I came to watch. You're gonna do good there."

Taking a step toward him so he could hear me without me yelling, I asked, "You came to my practice at Bryant–Denny? Why would you do that?" The man hadn't even come to the hospital when I'd broken my collarbone in little league. He wasn't exactly active in my life.

"I went to see both my sons' practices last week."

I froze. He'd called me his son. I started shaking my head. "No, no, you don't get to do that. I'm. Not. Your. Son."

I had to get away from this man. He was Sawyer's father; I did not want to hurt him. But *damn* if he was gonna call me his son.

"You are my son. I don't deserve you, but you are mine. You can deny me. You can hate me, and you have every right."

"Damn right I do!" I roared.

"It doesn't change the fact that I'm proud of the man you've become. The man you've become without any help from me."

I was taking loud hard gasps of air. What was he doing? Why was he doing this?

"Proud of me? Why? Because I can play some football? Because I'm playing at your alma mater? Because that's just bullshit."

Harris shook his head. "No, not because you're playing on the same football field I once played on, although that does make me feel a touch of pride. I can't help it. But this is only a brief moment in your life. The man you turned out to be is what makes me proud. You made bad choices and you got on the wrong path, but you were also strong enough to get off that path and find one that would take you somewhere in life. The world wanted to call you a loser, but you were so much stronger than they realized. You fought back. You grabbed the life you wanted, and you fought for it. Even when the rest of the world didn't think you'd make anything of yourself. You proved them wrong. That, son, is why I'm proud of you."

I wanted to yell from the top of my lungs at the unfairness of this moment. I'd needed this man when I was young and scared. *But now? I don't need him now.*

"A wise man once told me that you don't have to forgive me. You don't have to like me. But you need to know I love you, that I'm proud of you. All I needed to do was tell you. How you handle it or take it isn't what's important. What's important is that you know." He gave me a short nod, and the worry lines and defeated expression as he turned around to walk away made something inside my chest burn. I didn't understand this, but I didn't have to. Not right then.

"Harris," I called out to his retreating form. He stopped and turned back to look at me.

"Yes, Beau?"

I swallowed nervously, unsure how to say it exactly. Because his words didn't make this better. They didn't fix the past. "I don't know what to make of this just yet. I may never know what to make of this." I paused as a memory came to me of Harris standing at the fence during one of my high school football games as he thoroughly told off my coach after I'd been pulled from a game. I'd missed practice the day before because my mama had gotten sick with the flu and I'd needed to take her to the Urgent Care center in Mobile. It was the closest free health care clinic around.

I'd been put in the game once the coach walked back to the sidelines. Every time I glanced back at the fence during that game, Harris had been standing there with his arms crossed in front of his chest as if he was standing guard over something or someone.

"That game, in high school, when I'd missed practice the day before. I was benched. Then, after coach got back from a very heated discussion with you, he put me in the game." I stopped and studied his face and saw the answer in his expression. "You forced him to put me in, didn't you?"

Harris gave me a sad smile. "Wasn't your fault you had to take your mother to see a doctor. It was an unfair decision on Coach Madison's part, and I reminded him exactly how unwise of a decision it would be to leave his best wide receiver on the bench."

That didn't correct all the wrongs. But it did tell me that, at times, even if I didn't realize it, he had looked out for me. I'd just not known why other instances in my life had looked bad and then were suddenly okay with no explanation. Had it always been him?

"Coach wasn't a big fan of mine," I replied.

Harris raised one eyebrow. "Well, you weren't exactly the most dependable guy on the team."

I let out a short laugh. "I played just as good hung over as I did sober."

The smile on his face wasn't something I was accustomed to seeing directed my way.

"You probably did," he agreed.

We stood there staring at each other as if we were afraid everything would go back to usual the moment he walked away.

"Look, son"—he cleared his throat—"or Beau, if that's what you'd prefer I call you. If you want to go get something to eat sometime, or get a drink, or whatever . . . just call. I'll be there."

He turned and started walking away when I didn't respond. Before he got too far away, I called out, "You can call me son, if that's what you want."

Epilogue

Four years later . . .

SAWYER

"Come here, beautiful," I called out as I pulled off my helmet and held my arms open for Lana as she ran onto the field toward me. She was wearing her blue tank top with the Florida gator emblem. I knew the back of it read VINCENT #10. I'd had it made for her before my first game that season. She squealed and jumped up into my arms.

"You did it! You did it!" She rained kisses all over my face, and I enjoyed every minute of it as I held her up with my hands cupped on her tight little ass.

"Well, I did have some help," I teased.

Laughing, she ran her hands through my sweaty hair and kissed my forehead.

"I'm all nasty, baby."

She leaned back and looked down at me. A smirk appeared on her perfect, plump lips. "Yeah, you are."

What about that amused her, I had no idea, but it did. She looked to be on the verge of laughing about something. Then she grabbed my face and pressed those lips against mine, and I didn't care anymore. I just wanted this.

"Congrats, bro," Beau called out, and I opened my eyes as Lana let my mouth go. I slid her back down my body to stand beside me as I turned to see my brother walking toward me in crimson and white. Ashton was beside him in a jersey almost identical to Beau's.

"Thanks, man. You played good. That catch you made in the third was unreal. I had to keep myself from hooting on the sidelines."

Beau chuckled and shook his head. "I warned them that, although we whipped you guys the last three years, the best quarterback the SEC had ever seen would be starting this year."

Ashton let go of Beau to come over and hug Lana. It was our fourth year at the University of Florida. Ash and Lana talked several times a week. Beau and I managed to work out together on breaks when we were both back home. Beau even came to Christmas dinner the last two years. When he called our father "Dad" before leaving to head back to school after that first winter break, I thought our dad was going to break down and weep.

It hadn't happened overnight, but slowly Beau and Dad were finding ways to mend what was broken.

Beau was planning to propose to Ashton during the SEC championship game that year. The Florida Gators and the Crimson Tide would face off one more time this season. Other than us, no one else had been able to touch Bama that year. The plan was to have our parents there, even Aunt Honey, when Bama faced the Gators in the SEC game. "Will you marry me, Ashton Sutley Gray?" would be flashed on the big screen in the last quarter when only one minute was left in the game.

I'd had to listen to hours of Beau's planning and scheming. He wanted it to be just right.

I reached over and picked up Lana's left hand to kiss the marquis cut diamond that now rested on her ring finger. Our engagement, last month, hadn't been quite as big of a production, although it had made the ten o'clock news. After winning my first game as the starting quarterback for the Florida Gators, I'd bypassed all the media vying for my attention and gone straight to Lana as she made her way to me. The offensive line assistant coach had kept the ring tucked safely in his pocket during the game, but he'd placed it in my hand once the game was over. She ran into my arms like she always did after a game, but this time, instead of picking her up, I dropped to one knee. I'll never forget the look on her face or the way she sounded when she'd said, "Yes."

No longer was it me, Beau, and Ash against the world.

I had Lana, and she was the number-one player on my team.

ABBI GLINES is the author of *The Vincent Boys* and *The Vincent Brothers* in addition to several other YA novels. A devoted book lover, Abbi lives with her family in Alabama. She maintains a Twitter addiction at @abbiglines and can also be found at AbbiGlines.com.

Before Sawyer fell for Lana, he thought Ashton was his forever girl. Read Beau and Ashton's story in:

the vincent boys

ASHTON

Why couldn't I have just made it home without seeing them? I wasn't in the mood to play good freaking Samaritan to Beau and his trashy girlfriend. Although he wasn't here, Sawyer would expect me to stop. With a frustrated groan, I slowed down and pulled up beside Beau, who had put some distance between him and his vomiting girlfriend. Apparently, throw up wasn't a mating call for him. "Where's your truck parked, Beau?" I asked in the most annoyed tone I could muster. He flashed me that stupid sexy grin that he knew made every female in town melt at his feet. I'd like to believe I was immune after all these years, but I wasn't. Being immune to the town's bad boy was impossible.

"Don't tell me perfect little Ashton Gray is gonna offer to

help me out," he drawled, leaning down to stare at me through my open window.

"Sawyer's out of town, so the privilege falls to me. He wouldn't let you drive home drunk and neither will I."

He chuckled sending a shiver of pleasure down my spine. God. He even *laughed* sexy.

"Thanks, beautiful, but I can handle this. Once Nic stops puking, I'll throw her in my truck. I can drive the three miles to her house. You run on along now. Don't you have a bible study somewhere you should be at?"

Arguing with him was pointless. He would just start throwing out more snide comments until he had me so mad I couldn't see straight. I pressed the gas and turned into the parking lot. Like I was going to be able to just leave and let him drive home drunk. He could infuriate me with a wink of his eye, and I worked real hard at being nice to everyone. I scanned the parked cars for his old, black Chevy truck. Once I spotted it, I walked over to him and held out my hand.

"Either you can give me the keys to your truck or I can go digging for them. What's it going to be, Beau? You want me searching your pockets?"

A crooked grin touched his face. "As a matter of fact, I think I might just enjoy you digging around in my pockets, Ash. Why don't we go with option number two?"

Heat rose up my neck and left splotches of color on my

cheeks. I didn't need a mirror to know I was blushing like an idiot. Beau never made suggestive comments to me or even flirted with me. I happened to be the only reasonably attractive female at school he completely ignored.

"Don't you dare touch him, you stupid bitch. His keys are in the ignition of his truck." Nicole, Beau's on-again-off-again girlfriend, lifted her head, slinging her dark brown hair back over her shoulder, and snarled at me. Bloodshot blue eyes filled with hate watched me as if daring me to touch what was hers. I didn't respond to her nor did I look back up at Beau. Instead I turned and headed for his truck, reminding myself I was doing this for Sawyer.

"Come on then and get in the truck," I barked at both of them before sliding into the driver's seat. It was really hard not to focus on the fact this was the first time I'd ever been in Beau's truck. After countless nights of lying on my roof with him, talking about the day we'd get our driver's licenses and all the places we would go, I was just now, at seventeen years old, sitting inside his truck. Beau picked Nicole up and dumped her in the back.

"Lie down unless you get sick again. Then make sure you puke over the side," he snapped while opening the driver's side door.

"Hop out, princess. She's about to pass out; she won't care if I'm driving."

I gripped the steering wheel tighter.

"I'm not going to let you drive. You're slurring your words. You don't need to drive."

He opened his mouth to argue then mumbled something that sounded like a curse word before slamming the door and walking around the front of the truck to get in on the passenger's side. He didn't say anything, and I didn't glance over at him. Without Sawyer around, Beau made me nervous.

"I'm tired of arguing with females tonight. That's the only reason I'm letting you drive," he grumbled, without a slur this time. It wasn't surprising that he could control the slurring. The boy had been getting drunk before most the kids our age had tasted their first beer. When a guy had a face like Beau's, older girls took notice. He'd been snagging invites to the field parties way before the rest of us.

I managed a shrug. "You wouldn't have to argue with me if you didn't drink so much."

He let out a hard laugh. "You really are a perfect little preacher's daughter, aren't you, Ash? Once upon a time you were a helluva lot more fun. Before you started sucking face with Sawyer, we use to have some good times together." He was watching me for a reaction. Knowing his eyes were directed at me made it hard to focus on driving. "You were my partner in crime, Ash. Sawyer was the good guy. But the two of us, we were the troublemakers. What happened?"

How do I respond to that? No one knows the girl who used to steal bubble gum from the Quick Stop or abduct the paperboy to tie him up so we could take all his papers and dip them in blue paint before leaving them on the front door steps of houses. No one knew the girl who snuck out of her house at two in the morning to go toilet-paper yards and throw water balloons at cars from behind the bushes. No one would even believe I'd done all those things if I told them. . . . No one but Beau.

"I grew up," I finally replied.

"You completely changed, Ash."

"We were kids, Beau. Yes, you and I got into trouble, and Sawyer got us out of trouble, but we were just kids. I'm different now."

For a moment he didn't respond. He shifted in his seat, and I knew his gaze was no longer focused on me. We'd never had this conversation before. Even if it was uncomfortable, I knew it was way overdue. Sawyer always stood in the way of Beau and me mending our fences, fences that had crumbled, and I never knew why. One day he was Beau, my best friend. The next day he was just my boyfriend's cousin.

"I miss that girl, you know. She was exciting. She knew how to have fun. This perfect little preacher's daughter who took her place sucks."

His words hurt. Maybe because they were coming from him or maybe because I understood what he was saying. It wasn't as if I never thought about that girl. I hated him for making me miss her too. I worked really hard at keeping her locked away. Having someone actually want her to be set loose made it so much harder to keep her under control.

"I'd rather be a preacher's daughter than a drunk whore who vomits all over herself," I snapped before I could stop myself. A low chuckle startled me, and I glanced over as Beau sunk down low enough in his seat so his head rested on the worn leather instead of the hard window behind him.

"I guess you're not completely perfect. Sawyer'd never call someone a name. Does he know you use the word *whore*?"

This time I gripped the steering wheel so tightly my knuckles turned white. He was trying to make me mad and he was doing a fabulous job. I had no response to his question. The truth was, Sawyer would be shocked that I'd called someone a whore. Especially his cousin's girlfriend.

"Loosen up, Ash, it's not like I'm gonna tell on you. I've been keeping your secrets for years. I like knowing my Ash is still there somewhere underneath that perfect facade."

I refused to look at him. This conversation was going somewhere I didn't want it to go.

"No one is perfect. I don't pretend to be," I said, which was a lie and we both knew it. Sawyer was perfect, and I worked hard to be worthy. The whole town knew I fell short of his glowing reputation.

Beau let out a short, hard laugh. "Yes, Ash, you do pretend to be."

I pulled into Nicole's driveway. Beau didn't move.

"She's passed out. You're going to have to help her," I whispered, afraid he'd hear the hurt in my voice.

"You want me to help a vomiting whore?" he asked with an amused tone.

I sighed and finally glanced over at him. He reminded me of a fallen angel as the moonlight casted a glow on his sun-kissed blond hair. His eyelids were heavier than usual, and his thick eyelashes almost concealed the hazel color of his eyes underneath.

"She's your girlfriend. Help her." I managed to sound angry. When I let myself study Beau this closely, it was hard to get disgusted with him. I could still see the little boy I'd once thought hung the moon, staring back at me. Our past would always be there, keeping us from ever really being close again.

"Thanks for reminding me," he said, reaching for the door handle without breaking his eye contact with me. I dropped my gaze to study my hands, which were now folded in my lap. Nicole fumbled around in the back of the truck, causing it to shake gently and reminding us that she was back there. After a few more silent moments, he finally opened the door.

Beau carried Nicole's limp body to the door and knocked. It opened and he walked inside. I wondered who opened the door. Was it Nicole's mom? Did she care her daughter was passed out drunk? Was she letting Beau take her up to her room? Would Beau stay with her? Crawl in bed with her and fall asleep? Beau reappeared in the doorway before my imagi-nation got too carried away.

Once he was back inside the truck, I cranked it up and headed for the trailer park where he lived.

"So tell me, Ash, is your insistence to drive the drunk guy and his whore girlfriend home because you're the perpetual good girl who helps everyone? 'Cause I know you don't like me much, so I'm curious as to why you want to make sure I get home safe."

"Beau, you're my friend. Of course I like you. We've been friends since we were five. Sure we don't hang out anymore or go terrorizing the neighborhood together, but I still care about you."

"Since when?"

"Since when what?"

"Since when do you care about me?"

"That is a stupid question, Beau. You know I've always cared about you," I replied. Even though I knew he wouldn't let such a vague answer fly. The truth was that I never really talked to him much anymore. Nicole was normally wrapped around one of his body parts. And when he spoke to me, it was always to make some wisecrack.

"You hardly acknowledge my existence," he replied.

"That's not true."

He chuckled. "We sat by each other in history all year, and you hardly ever glanced my way. At lunch you never look at me, and I sit at the same table you do. We're at the field parties every weekend, and if you ever turn your superior gaze in my direction, it's normally with a disgusted expression. So I'm a little shocked you still consider me a friend."

The large live oak trees signaled the turn into the trailer park where Beau had lived all is life. The sight of the rich beauty of the southern landscape as you pulled onto the gravel road was deceiving. Once I drove passed the large trees, the scenery drastically changed. Weathered trailers with old cars were up on blocks, and battered toys scattered the yards. More than one window was covered with wood or plastic. I didn't gawk at my surroundings. Even the man sitting on his porch steps with a cigarette hanging out of his mouth and wearing nothing but his underwear didn't surprise me. I knew this trailer park well. It was a part of my childhood. I came to a stop in front of Beau's trailer. It would be easier to believe that this was the alcohol talking, but I knew it wasn't. We hadn't been alone in over three years. Since the moment I became Sawyer's girlfriend, our relationship had changed.

I took a deep breath, then turned to look at Beau. "I never talk in class. Not to anyone but the teacher. You never talk to me at lunch, so I have no reason to look your way. Attracting your attention leads to you making fun of me. And, at the field, I'm not looking at you with disgust. I'm looking at Nicole with disgust. You could really do much better than her." I stopped myself before I said anything stupid.

He tilted his head to the side as if studying me. "You don't like Nicole much, do you? You don't have to worry about her hang-up with Sawyer. He knows what he's got, and he isn't going to mess it up. Nicole can't compete with you."

Nicole had a thing for Sawyer? She was normally mauling Beau. I'd never picked up on her liking Sawyer. I knew they'd been an item in seventh grade for, like, a couple of weeks, but that was junior high school. It didn't really count. Besides, she was with Beau. Why would she be interested in anyone else?

"I didn't know she liked Sawyer," I replied, still not sure I believed him. Sawyer was so not her type.

"You sound surprised," Beau replied.

"Well, I am, actually. I mean, she has you. Why does she want Sawyer?"

A pleased smile touched his lips making his hazel eyes light up. I realized I hadn't exactly meant to say something that he could misconstrue in the way he was obviously doing.

He reached for the door handle before pausing and glancing back at me.

"I didn't know my teasing bothered you, Ash. I'll stop."

That hadn't been what I was expecting him to say. Unable to think of a response, I sat there holding his gaze.

"I'll get your car switched back before your parents see my truck at your house in the morning." He stepped out of the truck, and I watched him walk toward the door of his trailer with one of the sexiest swaggers known to man. Beau and I had needed to have that talk, even if my imagination was going to go wild for a while, where he was concerned. My secret attraction to the town's bad boy had to remain a secret.

The next morning, I found my car parked in the driveway, as promised, with a note wedged under the windshield wipers. I reached for it, and a small smile touched my lips.

"Thanks for last night. I've missed you." He had simply signed it "B."